Scanning the room, Buffy found the Ghost of Tara up at the front, staring plaintively out the window at a world she couldn't reach.

Buffy took a deep breath. "Tara, why didn't Willow do what she was supposed to?" she asked. "Why didn't she . . . stay to talk to you?"

The spirit took so long to answer that they all thought she wasn't going to. But finally the Ghost of Tara spoke. *"Because she is too angry now. There is nothing you can do that will make her obey, nothing you can do to make her trust you."* As Tara's gaze shimmered over everyone in the room, only Spike didn't shudder as it touched him. *"You should be very afraid now,"* the Ghost of Tara whispered. *"All of you. No one is safe anymore. Not even you, Giles."*

The librarian blinked. "You're serious," he said in amazement. "She would chance losing you just for the pleasure of killing me?"

The Ghost of Tara stared at him. *"There is your downfall,"* she told him. *"She won't kill you. But she'll make you wish she had."*

Buffy the Vampire Slayer™

Available from SIMON PULSE

Buffy
the vampire slayer™

Wicked Willow III
Broken Sunrise

Yvonne Navarro

**An original novel based on the hit television series
by Joss Whedon**

NEW YORK LONDON TORONTO SYDNEY

S|S|E

SIMON SPOTLIGHT ENTERTAINMENT
An imprint of Simon & Schuster Children's Publishing Division
1230 Avenue of the Americas, New York, New York 10020
™ & © 2004 Twentieth Century Fox Film Corporation. All Rights Reserved.
All rights reserved, including the right of reproduction in whole or in part in any form.
SIMON SPOTLIGHT ENTERTAINMENT and colophon are trademarks of Simon & Schuster, Inc.
Manufactured in the United States of America
First Edition   10   9   8   7   6   5   4   3   2   1
Library of Congress Control Number 2004102535
ISBN 0-689-86954-1

For:
Weston.
x3

Acknowledgments:

Thank you to Patrick Price
and to my husband, Weston Ochse.
Thanks also to all the Buffy and
Willow fans out there, without
whom this trilogy would have
never existed.
A special thanks goes to
Lisa Clancy, who kept
after me to do something
with the Wicked Willow idea.

Buffy the Vampire Slayer™

Wicked Willow III

Broken Sunrise

Prologue

Willow couldn't decide whether to be angry or devastated by the disappearance of the Ghost of Tara.

The past seven days had seen Willow run the full range of emotions: At first, she'd been patient, certain that this was only a temporary setback, that the Ghost of Tara had opted to bow out of the carnage of her awful battle with the Riley golem and was simply, as they said in the movies, "lying low." That patience had soon bled into stoicism and stubbornness—if the Ghost of Tara was going to be so touchy about the way things had gone that she wouldn't even make an appearance, then fine. It was kind of like waiting for a boy to call you after the first date: an anxious day of anticipation that soured into a defensive attitude of "I didn't like him, anyway" and the full spectrum of spiteful thoughts that went with it.

But of course that wasn't the sort of mental position that was going to hold for very long in Willow's life—not at her age, and certainly not regarding the spectral remains of her beloved Tara. Obstinance directed at the Ghost of Tara was nothing but a facade. It melted rapidly into despair, which turned into anger, which went back into despair, ad infinitum, until Willow felt stuck in the middle of an emotional loop—a brain-size, inescapable version of the wheels that hamsters were forever running on in their cages. Even the furious thoughts of revenge against Buffy, Giles, Xander, Anya, and Dawn had ultimately been overshadowed by her fear of the disappearance of the Ghost of Tara. Not forgotten—never that—but definitely relegated to the arena of "I'll get around to it."

Right now, Willow was at the tail end of another round of anger, and she was paying for it . . . yet again. This was at least the third time she'd repaired the damage done to her loft by her own furious hand, mending broken dishes and shattered lamps, organizing the double tier of spell books she'd swept onto the floor, rehanging the gauzy white material around the support pillars after she'd ripped it all down in a rage. And all that spent energy for what? So she could do it all over again when she decided to have her next temper tantrum tomorrow morning? How useless was that? Too much so, since it blackly assumed that the Ghost of Tara would *not* have returned.

Holding out one hand, Willow levitated the remains of a shattered stained-glass lamp, then let the pieces swirl slowly in front of her until they rearranged themselves as if new. A blink of concentration, barely noticeable, and the lamp was whole once more, giving off its warm, multicolored glow as she set it back in its place on one of the end tables. As beautiful as it was, she could find no joy in its colors or light. Even so, she wouldn't be so quick to smash the thing a fourth time.

Would the Ghost of Tara return tomorrow? Willow sank onto one of the floor-size cushions and cradled her forehead in her hands, trying yet again to pick her brain and her behavior and see what the hell she'd done to make the spirit run out on her. The golem? It couldn't be—that whole situation simply wasn't her fault. The root of the problem had been Buffy, as usual, who'd stupidly sent the golem after Willow and the rest of the coven, giving the creature the world's worst version of instructions. It would simply be too unfair of the Ghost of Tara to hold Willow responsible for the deaths of coven members Anan and Njeri, even if Willow herself had been the golem's initial creator. The Riley golem had been brought to life to *protect* Willow's coven, and it had been Buffy, not Willow, who had turned it against everyone. Why should Willow be blamed for that?

Or maybe it wasn't that at all; maybe it had nothing to do with the Riley golem or the two dead witches from her coven. Had she angered the Ghost of Tara with something else, by doing or saying something that had been, at least to Willow's mind, totally innocent? But *what*? What could make the spirit of the love of Willow's life utterly abandon her like this—no word, no touch, no inkling whatsoever of the faint essence of Tara upon which Willow had so come to depend on since the death of her lover's physical body?

Willow flounced back on the bed pillows and stared up at the loft's faraway ceiling, at the maze of duct work, pipes, and electrical wiring twined around one another in the heavy shadows. No, she was convinced she hadn't done any such thing, that it was just the Universe in its willful, twisted ways playing yet another wicked trick on her. How typical.

Abruptly, Willow sat up. She couldn't stand another night of this sitting around and just . . . *waiting.* She wasn't ready to give up on the Ghost of Tara, and certainly not on her goal of resurrecting the physical Tara—never that—but she had to get away from this loft for a while, be out with the people and the noise of Sunnydale, let the mundane little lives of others soothe her frazzled patience and the jagged edges of her nerves.

Yeah . . . an evening at somewhere noisy, crowded, and familiar—like the Bronze—was just what she needed to make herself forget the missing Ghost of Tara. Well, maybe not that, but she could leave behind the rest of the annoying problems that seemed to dog her at every turn.

At least for a little while.

"Hi."

Willow lifted her gaze from where she'd been contemplating the paper umbrella on the frozen strawberry margarita sitting on the table in front of her. The globe-shaped glass had been overfilled with the frozen sweetness, and now the drink was slowly melting, her lack of attention showing in the way the liquefying edges were just about to spill over the rim of the big, round glass. To her eye, the little multicolored umbrella looked downright ratty—it was faded and frayed at the edges, with the tiny, fragile structure of the umbrella bent in several spots, outright broken in another. Not very tropical, not very exotic.

Unlike the dark-haired girl in front of her.

She had shoulder-length hair that curved up at the ends and had in it brown swirls blending to shadowy black and framing a heart-shaped face with full, red lips and almond-shaped eyes. Her eyebrows were carefully arched, like a model's, and it was obvious that she'd given the same meticulous attention to her clothes as she had to her impeccable makeup. In short, the young woman was stunning.

"Hi," Willow said in response. "Am I supposed to know you?"

"My name is Lilith." The woman glanced pointedly at the empty stool on the other side of Willow's table. "Mind if I join you?"

Willow actually took a moment to consider the question, and ultimately decided that it all depended on Lilith's motives. The Bronze was a club, so a person's first inclination might be to assume the obvious: Lilith was on the prowl for a pickup, be it a temporary bit of company or something longer-term. In either case, Willow wasn't interested. Still, one of the many and more painful lessons that Sunnydale, with all its fine adventures and sundry inhabitants, had taught

Willow was never, *ever* assume. Besides, Willow was already thinking, just by the young woman's self-confident air, that Lilith was a person about whom she should learn a bit more.

On that note, Willow waved a hand toward the stool. "Lilith," she repeated. "Very nice." She looked down at the drink she didn't want, then brought her gaze back up to the woman sitting across from her. "They say that Lilith was the first wife of Adam—"

"And a female demon," Lilith finished for her. "Yeah, I've gotten the e-mail . . . a bunch of times. You know the one—it says the name means night monster, storm goddess, blah blah blah."

Willow couldn't help grinning a little. "Getting a little bored with it, I take it."

Lilith arched one eyebrow. "Only in the sense of day-to-day limitations."

Willow thought about this for a while without responding, and Lilith seemed content to order her own drink—something with cream and coffee-flavored liqueur—and wait out Willow's silence. Limitations. Interesting . . . she'd never really looked at it quite this intimately before, but limitations were what life was all about, weren't they? A constant search for the all-too-scarce freedom—in whatever form a person deemed it most important—and the will of the world to impose its rules upon that same elusive thing. From the moment a person was born, he or she struggled to be free just as hard as someone else—parents, teachers, bosses, lovers, spouses, whomever—fought to impose structure, a box within which you had to function or risk being beaten back into your place. And Willow knew that concept of place, all right—place was Sunnydale all around her, with its vampires and its supernaturally sodden history, its *pain*.

Its *limitations*.

There was Buffy and Giles, of course, and the rest of them, insisting that Willow behave within the rules set down by a sense of conscience and morality that was theirs, not hers. The same went for the Sunnydale Police Department and all the rest of the mere mortals who overpopulated this town; they just couldn't get it into their little brains that what Willow did was simply outside of their puny statutes and rulings. Even the vampires tried—unsuccessfully, of course—to impose themselves upon her, thinking ever so foolishly that she was just another tasty, juiced-up . . . what had Spike once said? Right: *Happy Meal with legs*.

And, most of all, there was this entire pesky Universe thing and how it challenged the resurrection of Tara. That was the most ultimate limitation of them all, and the most infuriating.

Willow's even-keeled mood abruptly faded, and she found herself straddling that edge again, the one where she might start hurling things around the room at any second. Except this time the room was a public place—the Bronze—and the potential flying objects were people.

Ah, those annoying limitations again.

"Why are you here?" Willow asked. She didn't try to disguise the sharpness in her voice.

"For two reasons," Lilith said, and Willow had to

give her bonus points for not waltzing around. "Rumor has it there's an open place in that coven you've got going. I know that a bunch of your members aren't there on a particularly volunteer basis, but I don't care." Lilith gave an attractive toss of her hair. "Personally I think they're missing the whole part about how it's a great opportunity to learn."

Willow kept her silence, although she knew she'd probably go on and let this woman join. Lilith wasn't a huge source of power, but there was enough there to add to the pot. Willow had felt it right away when Lilith had first pulled up her stool. "And the other?" she finally asked.

Lilith glanced around, as if she needed to make sure that no one else was within earshot. "I figure I ought to offer something to make my joining you a positive thing. What I have to tell you ought to at least put you on the high side of informed."

Willow frowned. "Informed about what?"

"Where that spirit of your girlfriend went."

For a moment, Willow couldn't do anything— breathe, think, blink, *explode.* And, as it turned out, there was no need.

Lilith wasn't stupid enough to play around with words on this most important subject. "There are a lot of stories flying around Sunnydale," the dark-haired woman continued. "Most of them are bogus, but I have a good ear for picking out the bull from the herd. There have been claims that she 'went into the light' and all that nonsense—can we say *Poltergeist*?—and just faded away into nothingness because you didn't get your act together in time."

Willow scowled and leaned forward over the table-top, but Lilith held up her hand. "Remember—I'm just the messenger here, bringing the free telegram. Don't bite my head off before I can read it to you."

Willow ground her teeth, then exhaled and sat back, waiting for Lilith to tell the rest of her tale.

"It took a bit of . . . convincing, but I finally managed to get the truth out of a guy I met at the scuzzy bar where the Slayer's been working. Yes, she's still there, putting up with the drunks and the barely there demon types. I don't know what she hopes to gain by it. So anyway, he wasn't much, just some kind of alter-dimensional demon who'd thought he was a badass . . . until, of course, he got to Sunnydale and found out what the word *really* meant. He had a lot of spite, but not much bite. I had to squeeze him a little, but I got the info." Lilith's dark gaze met Willow's, and suddenly the pathetic little umbrella in Willow's drink lifted into the air and spun lazily between them; then, in one sharp jerk, it crumpled in on itself and fell to the tabletop. "When I say 'squeeze,'" Lilith said softly, "I mean it literally."

Willow stared at the umbrella for a moment, then her frown faded and she smiled in spite of her building impatience. Sometimes the good stuff was worth waiting for, and sometimes the stroll on the way there was worth walking. "Excellent," she said. "I assume you can do more than just crumple paper."

A corner of Lilith's mouth turned up. "I don't mean to brag, but I do have my talents."

"Go on."

Lilith nodded, knowing full well that Willow wasn't talking about seeing more of her magickal capabilities. She folded her hands in front of her, interlocking the fingers as if she were praying. "Let's just cut through the pesky details and get right to the goods. According to this guy, Tara's spirit is being held prisoner somewhere in Sunnydale."

Willow sat up straighter and stared at Lilith. "Prisoner?" This was something she'd never considered, but now that it was out there, it made perfect sense. There'd been no reason for the Ghost of Tara to go stomping off, no argument or ultimatum—at least not this time. So why else would the specter disappear unless something or someone had taken her? And what possible good could come of swiping the ghost of Willow's dead lover? Who could possibly gain from that?

Willow ground her teeth.

Giles.

Chapter One

Willow's first inclination had been to head straight to the Magic Box and simply destroy it, bring it down with the biggest, baddest mojo she could think of, just pull it all down right onto their heads. In fact, she didn't just want to destroy the Magic Box, she wanted to utterly *decimate* it and everything and *everyone* inside it. After all, she was mighty tired of going over there time after time after time, just trying to get that old man and his has-been Slayer to back off and leave her the hell alone. She would pound that glued-together bunch of scavenged wooden pieces into nothing but toothpicks and use the bodies of the people inside—*all* of them—as the red glue to roll it into one tightly packed cube of splinters and human sushi.

But she couldn't.

Tara would never allow it.

Damn it—as Lilith had so unwittingly noted, there was that limitations thing again, and she had to keep this limitation as secret as possible. Okay, so it wasn't all that secret since most or all of the members of the coven realized it, but there was no need to place herself into a situation where it would be so blatantly obvious that it was the Ghost of Tara who was in charge, not Willow herself.

In the meantime, well, Willow was doing okay now that she knew the Ghost of Tara hadn't run out on her, and that she wasn't gone for good. Of course she missed the spirit's company, despite the fact that the Ghost of Tara was only a slightly stiff and off-kilter version of the real thing. But more importantly—and this was what had *really* terrified Willow—was that she needed that spirit to be present in order for the resurrection spell she was putting together to work. She just couldn't direct the energies properly if the Ghost of Tara was trapped somewhere. It had to be at least as free as it had been since its first appearance in Willow's loft and continual presence beside her and the women of the coven.

Speaking of the coven members, they were being quite cooperative lately.

Suspiciously so, in fact, considering two of them had been killed and almost all the rest beaten to within an inch of their Wiccan senses by the golem. It had only been about a week, but perhaps the best-behavior thing was because of the new addition of Lilith, but even that had to be a secret sore spot with Flo since Lilith could be viewed as moving into the place vacated by Anan. In any case, Willow would take it for what it was—a false calm—and watch her back. Lilith seemed like a good liaison, and the power that Willow was sensing from the dark-haired woman was greater than Willow had first thought, ranking pretty up there on the scale of what Willow had in her Wiccan pantry so far. It just went to show that Sunnydale was a lot further away from being tapped out than Willow had believed. The fact that Lilith had sought her out rather than been coerced into joining gave Lilith a sort of unspoken second-in-command status—a little bit of a competitive position with Amy. Perhaps that helped put the others on their guard, and on their best behavior all the time.

Upon reflection, why Giles had stolen the Ghost of Tara wasn't really that much of a mystery. The former Watcher shared the top culprit slot with Buffy, and again, it was about limitations. In Giles's case, "limitation" was just a synonym for "control." He thought by taking Tara's spirit, he could control Willow, and privately, Willow knew this was true . . . but only to a point. And when Giles felt it—and she guaranteed he would—that point was going to have a mighty sharp tip.

But this time, Willow decided she would try the milk-and-honey approach. They always had been suckers for someone they thought was trying to find redemption.

"I have a plan," Giles announced.

"Let's hear it," Buffy said. She caught movement

from the corner of her eye and barely stopped herself from going into a defensive spin. There it was again—the Ghost of Tara, just . . . *drifting* there. Buffy had liked Tara a lot when she'd been alive, but this version of her was just, well, *creepy.*

"Everything centers around Tara's ghost," Giles said.

"Please don't tell me that's the best your brain can do," Xander said from the other end of the room. He was holding a box of new merchandise while Anya emptied it, and Buffy could see his raised eyebrow all the way from her position.

Anya paused in her sorting of herb packets. "Difficulty concentrating is one of the symptoms of Alzheimer's disease," she said brightly. "I could concoct a brain potion if you're having trouble thinking. Fix you right up." She snapped her fingers for emphasis.

Giles pressed his lips together. "Thank you, but I'm certain my thought processes are doing just fine. Now perhaps you'll allow me to finish?"

Xander ducked his head. "Sorry."

"It's only a short while before Willow figures out we have the Ghost of Tara," Giles said.

"If she hasn't already," Dawn said.

"She might well already know," Giles agreed. "As such, we need to all know what we're going to do. Using the Ghost of Tara as the central ingredient to our success, I believe we can convince Willow to gradually relinquish certain key parts of her power as a sort of 'payment' for being allowed to visit with the spirit."

When they looked at him questioningly, he nodded as if to reinforce his position. "As each portion of her power is released, we then neutralize it so that she cannot regain that power."

"Wait a minute," Buffy said. "This is a person we're talking about—Willow—not a recipe where you whittle down the ingredients until you have what you want."

"Sure it is," Anya said smartly. "A recipe for disaster." She shot the librarian an exasperated look.

"No, it's not," he said stubbornly. "There's an undeniable logic to this—we have what she wants. If she wants it, she has to pay for it."

"Free enterprise and the American dream," Xander snorted. "Yeah, right."

"So you're aiming for what?" Buffy asked. "A powerless Willow? An oceanfront mansion on Maui?"

Giles gazed at her blankly. "Pardon me?"

"One's about as likely as the other."

"Thank you so much for your show of confidence," Giles said stiffly. "And to answer your question, no. I don't want Willow completely devoid of power. I don't believe we want a dried-up shadow of what she once was. I'd be satisfied if she just calmed down to the level of where she was before she drained Rack and me."

"And then what? You offer to finally give Tara back to her?" Anya had emptied the box Xander was holding and was now efficiently recording the last of its contents onto a clipboard. "Somehow I can't see this making her less pissed."

"My hope is that the loss of power will enable Willow's natural good spirit to once again be dominant," Giles explained.

"Fools."

Dawn yelped and stepped sideways in surprise as the voice of the Ghost of Tara whispered from right next to her. "Darn it, stop doing that!"

The spirit ignored Dawn as Giles turned to face her. "Why do you say that?" he demanded. "We'll make our demands small, like dismantling a tower one brick at a time. I can't imagine Willow wouldn't do anything to see you."

"See me?" A barely discernible smile pulled at the corner of the Ghost of Tara's mouth. *"You don't understand. Willow sees me all the time—in her heart, in her mind, in every single thing that she does. It's all an effort to bring me back. Your trouble isn't with what Willow might do to get my ghost back, but what she could do when she discovers she won't be able to get the* real *me back."*

Giles stared at the Ghost of Tara, a frown worrying across his forehead. "I could see where that might be a problem," he finally said, "especially given that she refuses to accept your prediction that it won't happen. When the time comes and it really doesn't . . ."

"Willow . . . ," sighed the spirit.

Someone pounded on the closed front door of the Magic Box.

" . . . is here."

Right from the start, she discovered she couldn't shimmer herself inside the Magic Box itself. If that wasn't enough for her to start sliding on her big plan to be reasonable and patient, she got an ugly zap on the hand when she tried to turn the knob. Then her mood went from irritated to downright furious when the blast of energy she directed toward the front door of the shop didn't work, and finally Willow began to hit the door with her fist, like a cop banging on someone's apartment door in one of those predictable television shows. The difference was that Giles had clearly put a repellent spell on it, and for her impatience, Willow got a triple zap of truly unpleasant electrical pain. The zing rocketed from the outside edge of her fist inward, flashing through her entire hand all the way up to her elbow before it melted away. With her planned diplomatic approach completely shattered, she had no choice but to stand back and wait until that has-been Watcher opened the door for her like this was no more than someone dropping by for a surprise visit. She was going to surprise them, all right. Oh, was she *ever.*

She had an energy ball of just about the size she wanted—massive—when the door was flung open. She pulled back to launch it and—

The Ghost of Tara stood in the doorway.

The fire-drenched weapon floating above her palm popped like a kid's oversize soap bubble. "Tara!" It was one of the few times that she'd used her dead lover's name when talking to her spirit, but the shock of seeing her after an absence of two weeks plus was great enough to cause the mistake.

The Ghost of Tara looked at her sadly but didn't move, didn't even lift a hand to reach out. Willow knew the spirit couldn't touch her—God knows, she had tried enough times—but the specter could have at least *reached*. Before Willow could blink, someone stepped between her and the Ghost of Tara, completely cutting her off from view.

That damnable Rupert Giles again.

Willow hissed at him like an enraged cat. Before she could bring back the energy ball, the old man held up his forefinger and shook it as though he were berating a naughty pet. "No, no, no," he said mildly. "Bad Willow."

"I will *kill* you!" Willow's words were nearly indecipherable through her gnashing teeth. "If you don't get out of my way, I'll turn you into nothing more than a pile of charred maggots!" She pulled her hand back threateningly, and suddenly it was filled with a ball of white fire.

"If I die," Giles said simply, "Tara dies with me."

Willow froze, then her eyes narrowed. "Give her to me, Giles."

"No." He folded his arms. "I am, however, willing to negotiate."

The fireball was still burning in her hand, but now Willow slowly closed her fist. As her fingers folded together, the ball shrank in on itself and finally disappeared. Her hand fell to her side, but Giles imagined it was like a deadly trapdoor spider, just waiting for the right moment to attack. "Really," she said. Her voice was flat and cold, completely emotionless. "Imagine that."

He nodded. "Obviously we have Tara. As you

doubtlessly just discovered, this morning I placed a very strong trespassing spell on the Magic Box."

"You did?" Standing a few feet behind him, for once Anya sounded impressed.

"Sure he did," put in Dawn. "Otherwise Willow would've already been inside for a toast and roast."

Xander scowled at the teenager. "You know, I really hate it when people talk about me like I'm an early bird special. There's just way too many menus in this town."

"I'd like to propose a trade," Giles said, ignoring their chatter.

On the other side of the threshold, Willow's face still remained impassive. Inside, though, she was *boiling*. Bad enough that this . . . this *librarian* had managed to prevent her from entering the Magic Box, as if she were some slimy vampire. Now he was going to make her *trade* something for the Ghost of Tara, as if the spirit were some kind of tacky little bauble on a sidewalk vendor's cart. Flaying? It was too good for him. Someday she'd turn him inside out and make him walk around Sunnydale like that for a couple of *months* before she finally let him die. But for now, he had started a game she was forced to play. "What do you want?" she asked.

He glanced over his shoulder, but none of the others said anything. "Spike," he said. "And Oz, too. Freed and brought to us here."

Willow's shoulders relaxed a little. Was that all? She wasn't going to let go of her poker face, but that was a small trade to get the Ghost of Tara returned to her. She'd miss Oz, of course, but Spike was just an annoying source of whining, recrimination-filled flesh. Good riddance—the loft would be a lot more peaceful without his constant crying and moaning.

"No problem," she said stiffly. "Give her to me and I'll see you get them."

Giles shook his head. "Oh, no. You bring them to us first and then you can visit with Tara's spirit for a bit. But you can't have her, not yet."

Willow stared at him, speechless. *"What?"* was all she could finally choke out.

"You heard me," Giles said with maddening blandness. "That's the trade. Take it or leave it."

"Visit with her?" Willow's mouth pulled into a black-lipped slash. "You think I'll accept this deal? Why should I?" Her hands were curling and uncurling at her sides. "Why *would* I?"

"Because if you don't agree, you'll never see the spiritualized version of her again," he answered. "You can even spend the next four or five decades waiting for me to drop dead, but when I do, her spirit is bound to me until *I* release her. No one else can do it. Not now, not ever." He looked at Willow steadily. "It's your call."

"All right." Willow heard herself saying the words, but she could hardly believe she'd been backed into such a position. It sounded like someone else, a stranger, asking the next question. "And after that? I'm not holding any of my Wiccans prisoner, if that's what you think. It's not like I can trade them like baseball cards."

"We'll talk about that at some future time," Giles said vaguely. "I'm sure we'll work something out."

"Fine," Willow snapped. "We'll *start* there." She almost added, *And just wait until you see where you end up!*—but then she really couldn't, could she? It was clear who owned the cards—or rather the *only* card—in the deal that she was being handed.

And with her best false show of pride, Willow lifted her chin and shimmered out of sight.

Chapter Two

She'd left the Magic Box in grand style, but that high-nosed exit held for only . . . oh, maybe three blocks.

Willow came back to her true form on the sidewalk and, unfortunately, right in front of an old lady who was wearing a ridiculous straw hat with flowers on it and pulling a loaded-up grocery cart. They ran full tilt into each other, and Grandma, whose well-fed bulk was definitely edging toward the two-hundred-pound mark, held on to her cart and her ground while Willow tumbled backward and landed hard on her butt.

As Willow blinked up at her from the cold concrete, the old woman gaped, then frowned and shook her pocketbook in Willow's face. "You ought to watch where you're going, young lady," she rasped. "You can't just be popping out of nowhere like that. Other people have rights, you know!"

Willow swatted the purse aside, getting a whiff of lavender and something else that was familiar . . . asafoetida? Not exactly the kind of ingredient the neighborhood block mother used in her chocolate-chip cookies. "Get that thing out of my face," she snapped as she pushed herself to her feet. "It's annoying."

The other woman glared at her, and now Willow could see that Grandma was younger than she'd thought, although still well into her golden years. Then, amazingly, the woman reached out and pushed Willow hard enough to make her stumble backward all over again. "Don't you talk to me like that, young lady! You mind your manners!"

Willow's mouth dropped open in amazement. "Are you *insane*? Touch me again and I'll turn you into an insect-eating toad!"

Grandma's eyebrows shot upward, then she reached up to finger something hanging around her neck—a polished piece of teardrop-shaped obsidian in a silver setting. "You just try it!" the old woman shrilled. The necklace was meant as a protection piece, and its wearer's next words revealed that she knew this. "You just try it and see what happens!" Great—was everyone in this town steeping themselves in magic? Apparently so, and Willow thought the result was like a lime left in a glass of water too long: bitter and undesirable.

Willow lowered her head and stared hard at the other woman. She was furious—for a lot of reasons—but one corner of her mouth picked up in a blackly amused smile. "Do you really think that silly little piece of rock will protect you? You have no idea who you're messing with." Willow made a sideways jerking motion in the air. The chain bearing the stone snapped, and the whole thing shot sideways and disappeared over the closest fence. She tilted her head and regarded Grandma dispassionately, like a guard dog considering which part of the burglar it was going to bite. "Do you have grand-children, *ma'am*?" She didn't wait for an answer, going ahead on instinct instead. "Wonderful. When you become a frog, I'll turn *them* into the insects you *eat*."

The woman gasped and let go of her cart, then began backing away, having finally decided Willow was perhaps a bite too big for her to chew. Willow watched her from beneath hooded lids, trying to decide if she really should make good on her threat. For the first time since leaving the Magic Box, she realized there was something on her face: moisture. God, here she'd been, crying and minding her own business, and this witchy old woman gives her a hard time just for bumping into her. No "Excuse me" or "Oh—sorry about that." Maybe she *should* turn her into a toad—one of those Madagas-car ones that looked like the Arnold Schwarzenegger of the reptile kingdom. And after that . . . frog's legs.

"I *do* know who you are!" the old woman cried. "That's right!" She'd abandoned her cart and scurried about twenty feet away, and now she raised her black pocketbook and shook it again. "And you haven't seen the last of me, either, missy—you just wait!"

Willow had just about decided to zap her, but well, what could she say to that? A challenge was a challenge, and this one had unintentionally saved Grandma's life.

"I'm looking forward to it," she said with deceptive mildness. "Say, don't forget your groceries." Before the woman could run, she sent the cart zigzagging toward her at an alarming speed; at the last second, she relented and hauled it to a stop in front of her.

"You'll just see!" Grandma yelled. She grabbed the cart's handle and jerked it nearly hard enough to overturn it.

Did she really need to bother herself with this old woman, use up her energy and attention? Not a bit, and by the time Grandma got things under control, Willow was already striding off in the other direction, reimmersed in her own problems. The wetness was still on her cheeks, and she hoped that Giles hadn't seen it— to him, it would be nothing but a chance for leverage, and she was pretty much at a loss already. She wiped her face and discovered that the side of her hand still stung, leftovers from the jolt of Giles's protection spell. Who'd have guessed the wannabe Watcher still had that much power—or the nerve to use it—after the hammering she'd given him? Then again, Buffy and her creepy crew always came back for seconds, thirds, ad infinitum. For some reason, they just never seemed to learn not only to save themselves, but also to leave well enough alone.

Well, Willow wasn't through with her lesson plan. "Mess with Willow 101" was going to have its first class this afternoon.

"That's good," Willow cooed at Oz. "Nice cranky puppy." Oz growled at her, of course—he always did— but there was the little matter of the raw two-pound porterhouse (no one could say she didn't feed her pets well) she was holding in her hand. Even a werewolf could be trained, to a point; he wouldn't exactly sit and offer his paw, but experience had taught him what to expect and he would go into a crouch and start drooling in anticipation. In wolf form, he was simply too stupid to realize she'd dosed the thing up with just the right amount of tranquilizers to make him docile enough to handle. The drug wouldn't last long, but then that wasn't her problem.

She threw it and Oz caught it in midair. Two pounds of prime Angus beef and it was wolfed—pun intended—down in just under four seconds. She'd hate to see what Oz could do to the human body if he wasn't tethered. Tsk, tsk. She puttered around the loft for a few minutes, and then, when Oz was calm and lying with his head on his paws, she walked over to him and wrapped a muzzle of invisible magic around his snout—obviously she didn't want him biting her, but it also wouldn't do to have him snap out at someone on the sidewalk. Werewolves were like the flesh-and-blood wild cards of the animal kingdom. That done, she went to Spike and yanked him to his feet— her impatience with all his blubbering was showing in her touch. He came willingly, watching with reddened eyes as she released the hold on the wall chain, then used it like a leash to lead him forward as she did the same to Oz. The werewolf growled low in his throat, but the drug had dulled his senses and the instinct to bite. He didn't exactly come willingly, but a steady pull on his chain kept him reluctantly moving. The sedative wouldn't last very long, but it would serve its purpose.

It was in fact kind of fun to lead the two of them down the stairs and out into the sunlight. Spike had to have a little special protection, of course, but that was no problem—the hooded cloak Willow draped over his shoulders was multilayered and a total sun block, so no part of his flesh was exposed. Even semi-insane, the vampire had the sense to hunker down and keep his face and hands covered. It was quite the walk to the Magic Box, and neither could she shimmer while dragging along both of them, nor just hail a taxi. Willow grinned at the looks she was getting—she must have looked like a goth girl swaggering down the sidewalk next to her own personal version of Death, and if Oz wasn't exactly Cerberus, he was a cool imitation. As a way to keep people from bothering her, he was truly the way to go.

Willow was almost to the Magic Box when she spotted Grandma again, sans shopping cart but still wearing that silly flowered hat. The old woman had the brains to stay the hell away from her, but Willow could feel her anger-filled glower all the way from across the street as she passed. Really, what was the deal? Had she really *meant* that little challenge? Surely the woman had other things to occupy her life. Time would tell; for right now, Willow ignored her and kept going, and Grandma wisely didn't follow.

She found herself getting angrier and angrier the closer she got to the Magic Box, and by the time she was standing at the front door, she was downright *seething*. How *dare* Giles make demands of her, and how *dare* he hold the Ghost of Tara hostage, a *tool* to be used to control her! Besides the fact that he was ignoring how much this hurt Willow, had the man even given a single thought to how Tara's spirit felt about this? Clearly not—Buffy and her nasty minions seldom thought of others. Willow had to make herself stop and stand there for a full minute while she fought to get her breathing and her temper under control enough to talk coherently. "Knock," she ordered Spike. "Go on. And keep your hand out of the sunlight, you idiot."

He peered at her from beneath the folds of his hood, and for a moment Willow thought he really didn't understand. But no—there was still someone home in that blond, spiky head, and he finally wrapped a layer of the cloak around one fist and pounded on the door.

Giles was the one who answered, of course, looking all English and tidy and wearing an expression of *I am so in control* that Willow was going to enjoy wiping off his face. For now, she'd settle for just being able to talk without having her voice shake with rage. "Let me see Tara," she said.

Giles looked from her to Spike and Oz, then frowned. "You have to change him back," he said, pointing to Oz.

"I want to see Tara," Willow said again.

Giles folded his arms. "First you do what I say."

"Fine," Willow said. She wanted to see Tara so badly—God, she did—but she'd had enough. She'd asked nicely, or at least as nicely as she could, and they were still digging at her, weren't they? Always snapping at the edges to see where her limit was, and hey, world, look out—Giles had just hit it. She would find another way to get her beloved's spirit back, but it wouldn't be like this, giving everything and begging for some little tidbit in return.

Willow thrust her head forward, and suddenly her eyes went from brown to black. Black veins writhed beneath the china-white skin of her face. "You think you can *push* me, old man? That you have enough power to order me around and expect me to behave like your personal well-trained dog? Well, guess what—this puppy *bites*!"

Oz's chain was in her right hand, Spike's in her left. She dropped both at the same time, and then, before anyone could react, she made a circular motion with her left hand that dissolved the werewolf's magickal muzzle, and yanked the protective coating completely off Spike's hunkered-over form.

Then she turned smartly and shimmered out of sight.

She held her shimmer until she could reappear inside the main part of her own loft. Empty, yes—no Wiccans until later in the day, and no Ghost of Tara, either. But that was all right too—it would come. Sure, Giles and the others would be angry, but they had those pesky things called consciences that would keep them from actually doing any harm to Tara's spirit. Buffy was the key player in there who would keep Oz from doing something disastrous, like killing Giles . . . although wouldn't it be funny if Giles got bit and ended up a werewolf just like Oz? After all, Oz's moonlight life had started with only a tiny bite on the finger from his cousin Jordy. Oz was likely to inflict a much more painful chomp, and Willow hoped Giles suffered for his sins against her—suffered a *lot*.

She let herself sink onto the thickest of the comfy chairs, then leaned her head back. She was so *tired* of everyone messing with her—it was bad enough that the Universe took Tara's physical body from her, but now her once-friends were keeping even her spiritual form away. Who wrote the rule that Willow couldn't have Tara, anyway? As far as Willow knew, only one person in the world and the Universe and anywhere in between had the right to lay that one down, and that was Tara herself. The one time that had happened, Willow had gone through a lot to get Tara to undo it, and damn it, she deserved to enjoy the results.

She closed her eyes and let her head fall back against the velvety softness of the chair's crimson-covered fabric. The deep cushions of the chair were so comforting and warm, inviting. A nap—that was the ticket. She hardly ever slept anymore, seldom even felt like it. Right now, for a change, she did want to sleep, just for a short while.

Long enough to dream about the damage being done back at the Magic Box.

Chapter Three

As soon as Willow disappeared, the screaming started.

It all happened so fast. Oz chomped on the thing closest to him—Spike—but the vampire was much more concerned about the overabundance of sunshine. He walloped Oz across the muzzle hard enough to draw blood, but it was really only reflex—Spike was well on the way to becoming a dust puddle on the doorstep. Oz snarled, then something must've snapped in his brain and made him realize he was actually *free*—a jerking look to the left and right, and he was off and gone.

The vampire screamed again, then Buffy knocked Giles bodily aside and yanked Spike inside. He hit the floor, then he was up again instantly. *"Hot!"* Spike cried. *"Hot, hot, hot!"* He was dancing around and flailing his hands in the air, shaking his head this way and that. Everything—his hair, his clothes, even his boots—was smoking, and a few exposed areas had bubbled to a hideous, painful-looking brown.

"Oh, calm down," Anya said. "You'll heal soon enough. At least we don't have to sweep you away in a dustpan."

Spike didn't seem to hear her, but at least he was calming a bit as it sunk in that he wasn't going to spontaneously combust. Finally he collapsed into a sitting position against one wall, choosing the floor over a chair at the table.

"Wow, that was a really *mean* thing for Willow to do," Dawn said. She was eyeing Spike mistrustfully, but there was a tinge of sympathy in her voice. "You know that had to hurt."

"Ow," Spike mumbled in agreement.

"Get over it," Buffy said roughly. She spun to face Giles. "We have a bigger problem right now: I've got to find Oz before he kills someone . . . or bites someone who gets away."

"Presto chango," Xander agreed.

"Life as a werewolf," Dawn said. "Hair on your palms and all over . . . other places." She shuddered. "Ew."

"It may take you a while to catch up to him," Giles said. He hurried over to the weapons cabinet and swung open the doors, then scanned down the impressive wall of axes, swords, knives, and the like until he found what he wanted. "Here," he said, pulling it free and tossing it to Buffy. "The tranquilizer gun."

"It's—"

"Fully loaded. Always."

She nodded and turned to go, then hesitated. Scanning the room, Buffy found the Ghost of Tara up at the front, staring plaintively out the window at a world she couldn't reach, obviously pining for Willow. "Tara," Buffy began hesitantly. It felt so *strange* talking to someone whose body she had seen lying in a huge circle of blood on the floor of her house. Sure, there'd been any number of spirits and creepies she'd had heart-to-hearts with, but this was different. This one hurt more, maybe because the pain and the effects of her death had reached so very far beyond the grave, and instead of fading, it just seemed to be growing worse and worse. Buffy took a deep breath. "Tara, why didn't Willow do what she was supposed to?" she asked. "Why didn't she . . . stay to talk to you?"

The spirit took so long to answer that they all thought she wasn't going to. But finally the Ghost of Tara spoke. *"Because she is too angry now. There is nothing you can do that will make her obey, nothing you can do to make her trust you."* As Tara's gaze shimmered over everyone in the room, only Spike didn't shudder as it touched him. *"You should be very afraid now,"* the Ghost of Tara whispered. *"All of you. No one is safe anymore. Not even you, Giles."*

The librarian blinked. "You're serious," he said in amazement. "She would chance losing you just for the pleasure of killing me?"

The Ghost of Tara stared at him. *"There is your downfall,"* she told him. *"She won't kill you. But she'll make you wish she had."*

Buffy grimaced. "That is so not the kind of prophecy I wanted to hear."

Xander swallowed and looked from Anya to Giles, then ventured his own question. "So . . . do you actually know what she's going to, uh, do to us? Like . . . specifically?"

The Ghost of Tara seemed to be staring at the ceiling. *"No. That part of the future isn't revealed to me. But I can feel her anger, even now, even though I can't be with her. Only Warren has tested her this badly."*

For a moment, they all digested this, then Dawn held up a hand. "Whoa—just hold on. As far as the majorly-wrong-things scale? We didn't even come close to what Warren did. Why should Willow be that ticked off at us?"

"I second that confusion," Xander said. Stress was making his voice a little loud. "Willow's the one who's done all the big bad mojo lately. Okay, so we might've had a little misjudgment in the way we sent that golem up to her loft, but *she* was the one who created it to begin with. It wasn't our fault it backfired on her."

The spirit's translucent eyes turned toward him, pinning him in place, unrelenting. *"This is not the way Willow sees it. Her anger has transferred from Warren to you—all of you. Yes, Warren took me away from her, but you are the ones keeping it that way."*

"This troubleshooting session is great, but I have to go," Buffy said. She grabbed her jacket off the back of a chair and shrugged it on, then jammed the tranq gun inside it as best she could. "The longer I stand here, the farther away Oz gets." She tucked her hair behind one ear and looked from Giles to the others. "As a survival method, the control-Willow bargaining plan doesn't sound like it's going to work. Maybe it's time to rethink it."

Giles nodded. "We've definitely got some things to consider. As for Oz, get him back here and we'll lock him up, then figure out how to break the perpetual moon cycle spell Willow's placed on him."

Buffy turned to head out the front door, then gasped when she came nose to nose with the Ghost of Tara. She'd damned near walked right *through* the spirit.

"Watch your step, Buffy." The spirit looked over Buffy's shoulder to where the others stared at her. *"And the rest of you, too. For Willow, there will be no reworking, no reconsidering.*

"It's far too late for that."

Five o'clock. The time when most of the good little worker bees of the business world were finding freedom from the daily nine-to-five. And the time, give or take twenty minutes, when Willow's own private little workforce reported for duty.

"We have a job to do," she told the other members of the coven. "But we're not going to do it here. I have a place—an abandoned underground tomb in one of the lesser-used cemeteries—that's been specially prepared." Maybe it was the tone of her voice, or the ghastly, rictuslike smile spread across Willow's face, but none of them seemed inclined to argue, or even venture a curious question or two. It was a blessed thing, a relief after so many obstacles and hindrances—she felt so on edge right now that she wasn't sure *what* she'd have done had she been faced with a fight from one of the women.

"Meet me here," she said, and pointed to a spot on a map of Sunnydale she'd unfolded on the tabletop. It was one of the cemeteries, but half of them hadn't even known it existed. "At the far back end. There's a dilapidated brick wall on the west side of the cemetery, and a run-down iron fence on the right. Follow the fence line to where it turns east and you'll see a mausoleum in that back corner. The whole place is like a forgotten world—I don't think there's been a caretaker there in years, and the last burial was probably more than twenty years ago." She looked at the other Wiccans meaningfully. "Even so, watch yourselves. You'd think being abandoned would make it the nonspot for hungry vampires, but it also makes it a tidy little safe haven for the bloodsuckers who want to avoid the Slayer." Her black smile stretched wider. "And don't forget that my boy Oz has gone all escapee. He's probably feeling hungry—werewolves always are—so it wouldn't hurt to arm yourselves with wolfsbane, salt, and protective pentagrams."

Sen looked startled, as if she'd just realized the reason for the sudden quiet in the loft. "Oz is out there?" She sounded absolutely terrified.

"Don't worry," Ena said soothingly. "We'll go in a group. And I know how to stop him, anyway."

"That's good," Willow said. "Just so long as stopping him doesn't have anything to do with hurting him permanently or killing him. Whatever's done to him I'll do to the woman who did it." She glanced around. "Clear?"

"Crystal," Ena said. Her voice was light, but Willow could tell she was frosted about it. Too bad— Willow would always have a soft spot for her very first lover.

"Anyway," Willow continued, "the name on the tomb is almost worn away, but you can still see it if you're looking for it—'Kiki.'"

"Sounds like some kind of Hawaiian princess," Lilith commented.

Willow shrugged. "Don't know, don't care. The tomb itself is mostly underground and empty. Maybe Miss Kiki turned out to be a vampire who went on her Hawaiian way decades ago. Inside the mausoleum is a staircase that leads to an underground chamber. There you will find a cave dug out of the back wall. It's a pretty fair size, and there's no other way out of it." Willow's eyes glittered. "It's just what I need." She spun the map around so that the rest of the Wiccans could see it, then stepped backward. "I expect to see every single one of you there in an hour." She snapped her Book of Shadows closed hard enough to make a few of them jump. *"Don't* be late."

Could a werewolf disappear from the face of the earth?

Of course not. They had no reason—no logic or thought other than to constantly kill and eat. Or maybe it was just kill, kill, kill—Buffy wasn't sure. In any case, Oz seemed to have done the magical *poof,* because she sure couldn't find him. Had he gone back to Willow's? Or maybe that had been Willow's plan all along, to make it look like she'd set him free when in reality she'd *poofed* him herself—right back into the chains by the fireplace in her loft. It wasn't inconceivable.

She'd been out here for a couple of hours, fast-footing it through the populated areas just to be a deterrent, shadowing the edges of the woods directly outside the more well-traveled areas, and downright prowling through the more thickly forested areas of the parks and wooded areas surrounding the cemeteries like a walking piece of juicy, human bait. But there was nothing, not even a paw print or a broken branch tipped with a bit of fur. Interestingly, there weren't any vampires, either, and that made her question her theory of Oz already being back at Willow's loft. Vampires were pretty fierce, but let's face it: They had a small mouthful of teeth and some good strength, but most of the time that fell apart when matched against the double muzzle of fangs, savagery, and bigger body of a werewolf. To Buffy, the bloodsuckers seemed to be in hiding . . . yet if she thought more about it, the reason for *that* was qualified because ever since the Wicked Willow "takeover," the vampires had taken care to lie low.

Oz was somewhere out there in Sunnydale, running free and lethal.

And Buffy would just have to keep on looking until she found him.

Chapter Four

It was a nasty demon and difficult to conjure.

Willow had found a reference to the creature by accident sometime ago. She hadn't been looking specifically for monsters—in fact she'd been skimming yet another ancient tome in search of a way to locate and take more power from all those pesky half, lower, upper, you-name-it demons that roamed the streets and secret places of Sunnydale at any given time. She'd nearly skipped over the next chapter, which had been given the juicy title of "Loathsome Creatures, Part 2," and it was that particular chapter's opening woodcut, detailed in truly ugly glory, that had come to mind when she'd first thought of revenge on Giles and the others.

Because this was a creature that was usually immune to spells and magicks, it would take all thirteen of them to do it. Willow had to wonder if it was actually worth the power drain—she could feel the energy being sucked out of her and into the spinning mass of blood-colored light in the midst of the pentagram they'd etched deeply into the dirt. In addition to the lengthy and complicated spell and all its components—herbs, stones, the dried skeleton of a small and nearly extinct flesh-eating fairy-demon—Willow had made each of the other women offer blood from cuts on their palms. At the end, she'd topped off their offering—as a sort of "icing on the cake"—with a double dose of her own life fluid, slashing her palm and shaking it over the almost-formed beast. The blood served two purposes: to provide just enough sustenance to give the demon life, and to forever identify those upon whom it would *never* be allowed to feed.

A *Gnarl.*

There were seven more pentagrams burned into the stone around the doorway, and these are what prevented this creature from getting out and feasting on the residents of Sunnydale. Willow knew the etchings were good and strong, and they would hold, but even so, when she looked at this beast . . .

Willow suddenly felt utterly terrified.

She couldn't explain it, but she *could* hide it, and hide it well. By the expressions on the faces of her fellow Wiccans, she thought they might feel the same way, but she knew instinctively that there was something else going on, some inexplicable link between her and this creature that she'd never encountered before. The beast itself didn't seem to notice, and that could only be a good thing. It wouldn't do at all for the thing to realize that the most powerful Wiccan in its world was afraid of it.

It wasn't particularly tall or burly. This thing was more or less shaped like a slightly-larger-than-average-size man, with skin that was a mottled greenish yellow and looked wet. Of course, it had a mouth full of extremely sharp teeth—didn't a thing like this, which was one of the building blocks of nightmares, always?—and evil-looking curved claws. Its scary face was a *loooong* way from *GQ*.

Even so, Willow waited tall and proud and fought against the urge to swallow as she stood face-to-face with the demon. Her heartbeat was uncharacteristically rapid, and sweat was trickling unpleasantly down her rib cage beneath her clothes. She hoped her breathing wasn't too telltale rapid, but she couldn't spare the concentration to make sure it was even—she had to focus everything she had on not revealing her terror to the Gnarl only inches away from her face.

"Why did you bring me here?" it asked in a hissing, singsong voice. It glared around the cave, regarding the other women—who were very obviously frightened—with narrow, almond-shaped eyes above its toothy mouth. Long lines of drool hung from its thin lips, and the thing rubbed the fingers of each hand together as though it couldn't wait for something to put between them. Willow resisted the urge to step away from the poisonous claws tipping its fingers—she must *not* show fear. "I'm hungry," it continued. "Yet you've kept me from feasting on the flesh of anyone present."

It almost looked sad. "Should have given me a birthday gifty, but there's none."

"You will eat," Willow promised. "But you will satisfy yourself only on those *I* allow."

The creature cocked its head sideways and seemed to smile at her. "So you'll be bringing me my meals? Such service. Oh, waitress, I'd like a menu, please." The word "please" came out *pleeeeeeease,* and Willow resisted the urge to shudder. It didn't help that the demon had a sarcastic attitude and liked to sing. Pearl Jam this thing was not. Sometimes it was better if they just didn't talk.

"Don't be absurd," Willow snapped. Her tone of voice had the gratifying effect of making the beast's sharp-tipped smile falter a bit. She gestured toward the pentagrams etched around the doorway. "Ever hear of 'Cinderella'?"

The Gnarl sneered at her. "A stupid human fairy tale, invented to scare small children." It flicked its poisonous fingernails in the air, making a series of nasty clicks with them. "*I* could give them this century's version of 'Hansel and Gretel.' Now *there's* something to truly be afraid of. Come out, come out, wherever you are!"

Now it was Willow's turn to find a dark smile. "There are many things one can learn from Cinderella." She turned and walked to the doorway, then passed her hand over the bottom-left pentagram. It glowed for a moment, then disappeared. "Six pentagrams," she said. "The magickal number is seven, and only seven will keep you imprisoned here." When the

Gnarl grinned wildly and looked about to leap for the doorway, she held up one finger. "But," she told it, "there are conditions. There are *always* conditions."

The Gnarl pulled back its lips in irritation, but paused to hear the rest of what she had to tell it.

"This missing pentagram is magickally tied to every Wiccan in this room." Willow swept her hand around, and the Gnarl automatically followed it, focusing on each witch, clicking its fingernails in anticipation as it turned. There were new faces here with Willow tonight, newly inducted Wiccans named Shira and Robyn, who looked anything but sure of themselves. They, especially, would need to feel confident in her methods. "I know about your poison," she continued. "Paralyze any one of us and it reappears—an added safety feature. Everyone here with me leaves tonight and no one but me ever returns. Should the seventh pentagram reappear while you are outside this tomb, you will be destroyed." The creature scowled at her. "In case you're wondering how, your internal organs will bubble out of your mouth and burn away. Your heart and brain will be the last to go, and you'll be alive and watching until the very end." She looked at the Gnarl steadily. "It will be super painful."

The Gnarl hissed, then ducked its head. "I get it," it said resentfully. "Humans have such a mean streak."

"Actually, you don't get it," Willow said. "Because there's more." She passed her hand over the blank spot next to the doorway, and the pentagram reappeared. "There are five names inscribed in the center of the pentagram," she told it. "You will touch no one but these five, and you will bring them back *here* to . . . feed." Willow couldn't help the slightest hesitation in her voice, and the gleam in the Gnarl's eye told her the creature had picked up on it. For now, the Gnarl said nothing. "No one else. And like Cinderella's carriage turning into a pumpkin, the pentagram will reappear all by itself an hour before dawn every night."

The Gnarl grimaced even more. "And after those five, is poor old Gnarl alive?" His out-of-tune voice dropped in tone. "Or does he starve, like a dying old dog?"

Willow's teeth clenched. Did she really intend to set this flesh-eating creature free in the world after it did her bidding?

No.

Hey, maybe she could turn it loose on Jonathan and Andrew . . . *if* she could only find them. In the meantime, she just needed to be careful about what she promised. Aloud, she said, "Start with these five, and I'll consider what to do next."

"Seems to be a bad deal to me," the Gnarl grumbled. "Five little meals, even if tasty . . . why should I agree?"

Willow's eyes darkened. This creature—no way was she going to trust it, not after so many things had gone wrong. It was better to go a different route, just to be safe. "Because that's the only deal you're getting," she told it. "In fact, I've changed my mind about something. You start with just one of those five—your choice—and then I'll have the rest brought to you . . . *if* you prove yourself." She paused. "Unless you'd like to just die now and I'll conjure up a different Gnarl."

Beneath its grossly hooked nose, the Gnarl pulled back its lips and ran a yellow-black, mucus-covered tongue over its lips, appearing to think it over, but only for a scant few seconds. "No need for hasty decisions," it hummed at her. "Perhaps once you see how good Gnarl is—*very* skilled, indeed—you'll realize how useful Gnarl can be."

Willow nodded, but her stomach was roiling uncomfortably—the thought of exactly what this creature was going to do suddenly didn't set very well. Of everything she'd done so far, *this* would definitely teach Giles and Buffy a lesson, but it would do it on a drastic level. But she couldn't back out now, couldn't show weakness. This had been her idea, and she had to follow through and stand strong in the eyes of her other Wiccans.

Giles, Buffy . . . whomever Gnarl found first. The creature would paralyze them, bring them back here, and slowly eat them alive. It was a horrible way to die, almost more than Willow could bear to think about. Still . . .

Willow hardened her heart, then passed her hand over the seventh pentagram and erased it. Without another word, the hungry Gnarl darted past her and disappeared up the stairs.

They shouldn't have taken Tara from her. They should have simply left her alone.

The coven went back to the loft en masse, opting for the safety-in-numbers thing. Not only was Oz still out there somewhere, but the other Wiccans had been totally creeped out by the Gnarl, prone to jumping at the slightest rustle of a bush by the wind or a night bird. Nothing Willow had said or could think of now seemed to make them relax, and really, she couldn't blame them. All she wanted was to put it out of her mind. She'd made a decision and started her plan. Now it was just a matter of sitting back and watching things unfold.

Her beautiful building glowed in the darkness, like a cube of swirling blue ocean in the midst of the ugly industrial park. It was a welcoming sight, and as soon as everyone had gathered up the personal items they'd left at the loft earlier, she would finally be able to kick back and rela—

"You!"

Willow had been just about to shimmer upstairs when the shrill yet familiar voice jerked her concentration out of whack. The break in focus stopped her from going anywhere and gave her a zingy little pain in each temple. She took a step backward instead, then blinked and looked toward the sound of footsteps clomping toward her.

"Oh, I should have *known* you'd have something to do with it! You think you're so smart, you with your ridiculous black lipstick and fingernails and clothes!"

Great—just like she'd thought, that voice belonged to the woman she'd bumped into after coming out of the Magic Box. Grandma was stomping toward her, but her wrath wasn't aimed just at Willow. Her glare took in several of the other Wiccans who hadn't had the good luck to get the hell out of there before the elderly woman's arrival.

"What are you talking about?" Willow demanded. "Something to do with *what*?"

"The disappearance of my granddaughter, that's what!" Before Willow could think of a counter to this, the woman poked her in the shoulder with a hard finger. "I want to know where she is, and I want to know right now!"

"Hey, cut that out!" Willow slapped the woman's hand aside as it came in for another jab. "I don't even know who your granddaughter is. Why do you keep showing up in my life, anyway?" For the first time, Willow realized that Grandma had brought reinforcements, towing along a man who might have been her husband—his age was hard to tell—as well as a dowdy-looking middle-aged woman with dull, dyed red hair. Her adult daughter? While the man had an *I don't believe this is happening* expression on his face, the younger woman looked as hostile as Grandma herself. Did she know these people?

"Where's my daughter?" the redhead cried. Her voice was startlingly loud. "Megan said you were making her work for you, that she was afraid to try to quit. What are you doing in there? Drugs? Or worse things?" She shook her fist under Willow's nose, already a replica of her mother although she was twenty-five years younger.

Willow gaped at her, completely thrown. She should have seen this coming, should have made some sort of . . . provision for it or something. Megan—and Dilek, too—were still somewhere in the great unknown of the globe, thanks to good ol' Giles. Willow wasn't even sure they were still *alive,* although based on what had happened to Flo and how long they'd been gone, she sure wouldn't have put a lot of money on it. Dear God, what was she going to tell Megan's family? Could she actually lie to them, face-to-face?

Before she could try, Lilith stepped smoothly in front of her. "She did work with us, yes," the black-haired woman said in a honeyed voice. "But we haven't seen her in . . ." She looked over at the others, needing a time frame.

"At least a week," Amy said suddenly. "I couldn't say for sure." She shrugged. "We didn't miss her because it was pretty obvious she wasn't coming back." She glanced at Willow, who snapped her mouth shut and let them take the lead. In an offhanded way, she was pretty impressed (and maybe a little concerned) by Amy's lying skills, but now was not the time to be worrying about that. "She could've left anytime she wanted," Amy continued. "I don't know why she'd say something like that."

Megan's mother thrust her chin forward. "Are you calling my daughter a liar?"

"Of course she's not," Lilith said. "I'm sure Megan had her reasons for whatever she decided to tell both of us."

Megan's mother frowned, but she couldn't quite follow Lilith's logic. She turned away, giving Willow a hateful glance out of the corner of her eye. "Don't know why she kept monkeying around with that ridiculous hocus-pocus crap, anyway. Just made her prey for crazy people like you. She knew what I thought about it all."

Willow started to say something in reply, but Grandma's harsh voice overrode her. "You should've had a little more faith in your daughter, Brenda," she insisted. "Maybe then she would've confided in you and Drake."

Megan's mother—Brenda—rolled her eyes. "Oh, don't start that again. Twenty-first century, remember? People don't pop in and out of space, and they don't fly around on broomsticks, either. For God's sake, Mother, would you get a grip already?"

But Grandma only snorted. "Now you see why Megan spent more time with me," she said haughtily. "This town is infested with people like *her*." She jabbed a finger in Willow's direction. "Bad women who have the wrong influence on good girls like Megan."

"Hey," Willow said hotly, "let's not get personal here. You don't even know me."

"I know all I need to," Grandma retorted. "Except where my granddaughter is. If you think you can hide the bodies, you're in for a big surprise."

"Bodies?" Willow stared at her. Her mouth had suddenly gone dry.

"Figure of speech." Up to now, the father—now Willow could finally assume he belonged to Brenda— a haggard-looking man who was thin and had even thinner amounts of hair, hadn't said anything. In fact he'd had such an exaggerated air of patience that

Willow had offhandedly wondered if he wasn't one of those "peripheral parents" who orbits around the family in an ever-widening circle of disinterest. "I say we call the police, like I wanted to do from the very start. We've let this go on way too long already."

"Well, I don't care if either one of you believes me," Grandma said stubbornly. "I know what I can do, and what Megan could do." Her eyes narrowed as she focused again on Willow. "And what *you* can do."

Willow was getting tired of this. "Oh, you have no *idea* what I can do," she said ominously.

"Tell you what," Lilith said smoothly. "Why don't we give it a few more days. Megan was pretty introspective. She didn't tell the rest of us much about what was going on in her home or social life. I'm sure she'll work out whatever she's going through and will be back soon."

"Oh, aren't you just the silver-tongued she-devil?" Grandma's face twisted. "Do you really think I'm falling for this crap?"

"You've got two days," Megan's father said suddenly. He got a hand around each woman's wrist and tugged them backward. "Two days. And then we're going to the police. See if you can sweet-talk them like you *think* you're doing us."

"I'm not—," Willow began, but Lilith cut her off by steering her away from the family.

"We'll be back," Grandma promised. "And next time, you won't be brushing us off so easily."

Willow resisted the urge to say she'd be doing a whole lot worse, and let them go. The creation of the

Gnarl had been incredibly taxing, and now this. She hadn't a clue how to find Megan or Dilek, or, for that matter, how to explain the disappearance—deaths—of Anan and Njeri, and after what she'd started tonight, it was unlikely Giles was going to be any help. She should have foreseen this, made some provision for the angry friends and families left behind. She never swore anyone to secrecy—frankly, she just hadn't been scared enough of anyone to care—so if Megan's family knew about Willow and what she was doing, then it stood to reason that the others had told their relations too, perhaps lovers, friends, siblings. How many people could be involved here, how many generations?

So what the hell was she going to do when Megan's family—or anyone else, for that matter—came back?

Chapter Five

At the back of the newly renovated Magic Box—which sounded like so much more than what really had been done—was a little antique clock. To say it was a cuckoo clock would be almost right . . . but a whole lot wrong, too. It was small, just like the little Swiss clocks seen in a thousand old black-and-white movies, but what came out of the tiny door at the top of every hour was anything but a chirpy sounding bird sculpture. Anya thought birds were annoying, so about four months after she'd gotten the thing, she'd pitched the wooden one that came with the clock and replaced it with a cave sprike, a two-inch-tall creature that looked like it was part albino lizard and part mutated firefly. She'd permanently clipped its wings so it couldn't fly off, then put a spell on the clock itself so that when it was supposed to chime, it fed the sprike a worm instead. Each time a cave sprike finishes eating, it makes a soft, exquisite shrieking noise that sounds a lot like the scream of a man being punished for his infidelity. It was one of the few things that had survived the Wrathful Willow carnage, and Anya just loved it. She looked forward to hearing it every hour, on the hour. She had a nice afternoon routine going that included the clock, Xander's postwork appearance at the Magic Box, and the ritual planning of her evening—what she and Xander would eat, where they would go, if they would fight demons or vampires or just go to one of their apartments and watch television. If anything came after that, well . . . who knew.

Which was why she knew something was wrong when the four o'clock shriek came and went and no Xander.

"Well, that just figures," she said out loud. There was no one else to hear her, but a thousand years of living had long ago taught her the value of talking to herself. "He's probably out having a manly beer with the sweaty guys he works with." Perfectly plausible, even expected, except that she was sure they'd talked about getting a pizza tonight, maybe even renting some innocuous movie—something *without* monsters, thank you very much—and eating microwave popcorn until midnight. After all, a lot of the baddies around Sunnydale were lying low, an unexpected but welcome side effect of the reign of Willow.

Yeah, they'd definitely had those plans, and it wasn't like Xander to forget them or just blow it off. Now that she thought about it, they'd even picked the tape—not a movie, but one of a series they'd seen at the video store, a British series called *Fawlty Towers,* something that was supposed to be hilarious and of which she'd only caught a couple of scenes. She'd been planning to ask Giles exactly why the Brits thought a woman saddled with an inane and completely inept husband was so funny, but Giles was off at some estate sale prowling through the books of some dead, secret sorcerer and trying to convince the man's executor to sell him the whole lot before someone with unsavory ambitions showed up and outbid him. At least *he'd* called.

Still, Xander was swinging free and loose now—what claim did she have on him? What right did she have to complain if he decided a beer with a bunch of overly loud men was more important than her? She couldn't even say he wouldn't do such a thing, not for sure, because who would have ever thought he would take the vengeance-induced visions of one of her past victims to heart, blowing it all out of proportion—at least to her mind—and using it as a reason to leave her at the altar?

Boy, that still stung.

But . . . he *had* been looking forward to tonight.

So where the heck was he, anyway?

It had all happened so fast.

One second, Xander had been thinking about stopping to get Anya a gift on the way home—nothing complicated (she liked Butterfinger candy bars)—and the next, he'd been in the bushes. He'd decided to drop his car off for an oil change and pick it up in the morning—after all, he and Anya were up for an evening at the apartment tonight. The Parks Department would probably have to cut all the bushes in Sunnydale down before people would remember not to walk right next to them, even in broad daylight. Sometimes he was like all the rest of Sunnydale's residents. He just didn't seem to be getting the memo about Sunnydale being an evil, evil place and that afternoon daylight did not necessarily make any difference.

And boy, this was about as evil as it got.

The thing that had grabbed him was definitely a demon, but Xander couldn't get a clear look at it. All he knew was he was dragged to a cave or tomb or something underground, and the demon kept moving around just outside of his field of vision, circling him like a hyena pattering around an injured zebra. The creature had done something to him, right when it had grabbed him, because Xander was utterly paralyzed. At first he'd been able to make his lips move, but now he couldn't move a single thing except his eyeballs and eyelids and, oh yeah, his tongue. He could sort of make talking sounds, not that the demon was actually listening. He'd read somewhere once that no matter how serious the paralysis, people could always move their eyes and blink. Even Giles had still been granted the minor necessities of life, like being able to move his upper body, turn his head, scream for help—yeah, little things like that.

On the flip side, maybe the paralysis was a good thing, because the demon, who sounded so absurdly happy that it was literally humming to itself, was *doing* something to him.

Xander couldn't actually feel it, but he could see it. Well, sort of. Every so often the thing would walk around him, muttering and mumbling to itself, not actually talking right to him—yet—then it and its pointy ears and walrus-length nose would pass out of his field of vision. It was that same field of vision that would then start to *shake,* as though the demon were pulling on him or something. Very strange.

And later the demon rummaged around in the blackness and came up with a torch. Firelight blazed through the darkness, making Xander's eyes water. When his eyesight finally adjusted to the new level of brightness, he got an eyeful of his captor for the first time. Pretty ugly, but par for the course—a lot of the demons looked alike, with a tendency toward strong, skeletal builds and lean bodies, ugly skin, watery eyes, plenty of teeth. It was like somebody in the Hellmouth kitchen followed a pretty standard recipe for disaster. The question was always just exactly what did your particular demon have in his beastly little arsenal. This one had apparently been given the ability to paralyze its victims. But for what reason?

Xander's line of sight didn't include much beyond a circular view of the roof of his prison and a little bit to each side. When the demon had dropped him on the floor, then repositioned him, somehow his head had gotten tilted back slightly, just enough so that if he strained, he could see the tip of his own nose but nothing much else. The rest of his body was as much a mystery as Einstein's Theory of Relativity. That's why, when his vision shook for the third time and the demon actually bent into his field of vision and spoke to him, Xander was pretty damned surprised.

"Tasty," it said to him with a bloody smile. "Very, very tasty." Xander's eyes widened—at least he thought they did—when the creature held up something long and wet-looking. It was red and white, and obviously a strip of fresh skin.

His *own* skin.

In his mind, Xander's scream went on for a long, long time.

Of course, Anya suddenly thought. *He's helping Buffy track Oz.*

It was such an obvious explanation. It still stung a little that he hadn't called, but at least it was a better than beer.

The problem was that when Anya went to the weapons cabinet to check, only one of the tranquilizer guns—the one Buffy had taken—was gone. They'd all done their share of silly things, but Xander wasn't about to go werewolf hunting without carrying werewolf-specific weaponry. So much for the great Oz hunt theory.

Thoroughly aggravated now, she yanked the feather duster out of the closet and started working furiously on the shelved merchandise. Maybe he really *had* chosen boys and beer over their little movie date, and while she might think it was rude, she really couldn't do squat about it. The annoying truth about their relationship—assuming what they had was actually such a thing—was that she no longer had a claim on him. Now they were just dating, just like way back before the "I love you" and the "Will you marry me?" The whole thing left her feeling really bitter and sorry for herself.

She'd worked her way halfway around the shop, barely managing not to break anything with her angry swipes of the duster, when she heard the front door open. She whirled so quickly, she nearly took a small stained-glass globe off the shelf with the handle. Good reflexes let her catch it, thank goodness—it was said to contain the seeds of a plant that would protect the person who broke it against certain types of fungus-related spells. No sense in wasting that, and besides, the seeds were very expensive, even at wholesale.

"Xander?" She tried to sound bright and happy, but even to her own ears, her voice came out angry. She tried again as she headed toward the front. "Is that you?"

"Not the last time I looked," came Buffy's reply.

"Oh, it's you."

"So happy to see you too." Buffy peered past her. "Have you seen Dawn? Or Giles?"

"Giles is off at some book auction, trying to cut yet another deal. You'd think he was still a librarian, or a Watcher." Anya gestured at the packed shelves and the books scattered across the worktable. "I don't know where he thinks I'm going to put this latest collection if he gets it."

"Once a bookworm, always a bookworm," Buffy

said, but even she felt a pang at that. Willow used to refer to herself like that, but the subject matter of her precious books had changed drastically. She focused back on Anya and looked at her hopefully. "Did you say you'd seen Dawn?"

"I did not," Anya said. "And I haven't." After a moment's silence, she added, "And I haven't seen Xander, either. Do you think they're together?"

Buffy frowned. "Without letting one of us know? Doubtful." She glanced at Anya's macabre clock, ignoring the ghastly little thing that sat and preened itself just inside the hole in its upper half. "It's almost five—she should have been home an hour ago."

"Maybe she went out with some of her friends," Anya suggested. "Socialization is very important, you know. Especially during the formative teenage years."

"Maybe she ran away," Spike suddenly suggested, startling them with a moment of lucidity. "Happens all the time, you know."

"No," Buffy said. "We're not doing milk cartons. Dawn knows the rules. If she decides to go somewhere after school that's not home, she has to call." She held up her cell phone. "As of now, I am ringless."

Anya reflexively looked at her left hand. "Me too," she said sadly.

Buffy decided not to get into that. "Any ideas where they could be?"

Anya blinked and tried to refocus her thoughts. The only thing she could think of—still—was Oz. "Werewolf tracking?"

But Buffy shook her head. "No way. It's far too

dangerous. Xander knows that, and Dawn would never try something that insane, wacky teen hormones or not. Have you listened to her talk about Oz? She has a nice, healthy fear of having hair on her chest. She wouldn't go near him."

"Too bad we can't say the same for him," Anya said, then regretted it as soon as the words left her mouth and Buffy stared at her in dismay. "Oh, I'm sure she's fine," Anya added hastily. "I mean, she's smart and savvy. She knows to avoid all the places around Sunnydale where the life-threatening monsters hide." She hesitated. "Doesn't she?"

Buffy's eyes were shadowed with sudden worry. She looked over at Spike, but he was no help. He'd already lapsed back into his self-absorbed mumbling. For heaven's sake, wasn't he ever going to do anything but sit in the corner and whimper ninety-five percent of the time? Sure, guilt sucked, but if you wanted to make yourself feel better about the crappy stuff you'd done, you had to be proactive. Angel was a prime example of that, but the only thing Spike seemed good for right now was as a case study for a psychiatric student's master thesis.

"Hey," Buffy said abruptly. "Where's the Tara ghost?"

"Good idea!" Anya scanned the room. "She'll know something. She can probably see where they are right now . . . except"—Anya's brow furrowed—"except we can't see *her*."

Buffy's footsteps took her on a rapid tour of the main room. "She didn't somehow get away, did she?"

Anya shook her head. "No. I can sense her in here somewhere—"

"Over there!" Buffy pointed a finger up by the front door. She started to stride over there, then hesitated. "Wait a sec. Why is she . . . *crying*?"

But nothing they could say would convince the Ghost of Tara to talk to them or meet their worried gazes.

Chapter Six

The first thing that hit Willow was the smell.

She'd breezed into the cave with her head held high and her haughty-meter in the overload zone, like a dark princess gracing the prisoners in her dungeon with a glimpse of her royal presence. Such a childish notion, and it rightfully dissolved the instant the torchlight the Gnarl had placed around the cave served to open her eyes. This was a serious, serious thing she had done, and in the world she had now made for herself—and others—there was no more room for juvenile fantasies.

Blood.

The air was thick with the scent. There were a thousand, maybe tens of thousands, of stories and books in the world where the writers waxed poetic about the "copper scent of blood." Well, there was nothing remotely copperlike about the air that assaulted her nose now, and in real life, decaying blood smelled like rot, not copper. Along with that was the clichéd phrase "the sweet scent of decay." Again, there was *nothing* sweet about it—it was ripe and sickly, overwhelming, and unless you'd taken a one-way trip into the vampire gene pool, it usually made you want to vomit. Tonight was no exception.

The Gnarl had put Xander at one end and Dawn at the other, foot to foot. It had ripped Xander's shirt off him and flung it into a corner, then gone to work on the skin covering the nice six-pack of abs that had once caught Cordelia's eye when Xander had tried out for the swim team at Sunnydale High. Now Xander's stomach was an open wound that was slowly seeping blood down his sides and into the dirt. Like Dawn, he lay there completely helpless while the demon took its time eating him alive.

The Gnarl had taken Dawn's blouse off, but had forgone her stomach in favor of the skin along her collarbone. Her sports bra was crimson with blood, and her wide eyes were focused on the ceiling, and maybe on some better place in her mind—the mall, perhaps, where she should have gone. As Willow understood tonight's events, she'd gossiped a little too long with her friends, then decided to cut through one dark alley too many. Sunnydale was full of them. Dawn, meet the Gnarl. Gnarl, meet your second course.

All the soapbox speeches Willow had been planning burst apart in her mind like a dud fireworks display. It was bad enough to see Xander and Dawn like this, but there was more—like an uncomfortable . . . *buzzing* inside her brain. Some kind of warning, or sixth sense? Would this beast turn on her like the others had? No, she'd taken too many steps, used serious won't-be-fouled-up caveats, for that to happen. Still, what was it about this beast that shook her all the way down to her soul? It was almost like a prophecy, but that was ridiculous, because she'd never been one to get those. She wasn't the queen of the indecipherable dreams of doom; Buffy was.

The Gnarl was sitting on the ground against the far wall. Its legs were stretched out in front of it with its ankles crossed, and its hands were folded lightly across its belly. Had its stomach been rounded, it would have been the perfect picture of contentment after an oversize meal. Instead it had more the look of a predator digesting the first round and ready to come back for more.

Willow circled Xander and Dawn, trying not to breathe their predeath scent. There was a lump in her throat the size of a softball, and she had no idea if it was from fear of the creature or fear for Xander and Dawn, for what they were going through. Thank God for the paralysis—they were feeling none of the pain when each small strip of their flesh was peeled away. They couldn't move, scream, or even cry. But Willow couldn't help wonder what was going on in their minds as they watched themselves being eaten.

"Gifties," the Gnarl said placidly.

Willow turned, startled. "What?"

"Gifties," it repeated. He lifted one arm lazily and

pointed at Xander and Dawn. "Good gifties. You picked good ones for me. I even did something different and started from the top with the second one instead of the belly. Very nice."

Her teeth were involuntarily clenched together, so Willow didn't say anything for a moment. When she could finally speak, she made herself inhale, then step toward the demon. "There are more . . . *gifties* waiting for you," she said.

Surprisingly, the Gnarl shook its head. "Oh, no. One gifty is good, two is great. Three is one gifty too many. I can only eat so many at a time. I get too full. Will have to get other gifties later, after these are done."

"Stp."

Willow gasped and whirled. "Dawn?"

The teenager was still in the same prone position, still had two dozen or more horrifyingly bloody strips missing from the formerly smooth expanse of her upper chest, but now her brown eyes were straining to the side, just able to focus on Willow. As Willow stared, a tear leaked from one corner of Dawn's left eye and slid downward to disappear into her hair. "'Lo, plez hlp uz."

"Be quiet!" Willow cried. God, she hadn't realized they could talk, or cry—she hadn't known she was going to have to deal with that!

The Gnarl sat upright. "Sorry, witch lady. They usually quiet. Too full now, but later I can eat the tongues to keep them quiet, if you want. Don't usually like—too tough—but for you, Gnarl will do it."

Willow shook her head. Oh, no—no, no, no. She wasn't going to be able to deal with this much detail, this much *gore*. "Don't bother," she said with as much carelessness as she could manage. "I was just startled, that's all." She thought she heard Xander say something, but she blocked it out. "So you don't want another . . . gifty?" The word and all its implications made her want to gag.

The Gnarl shook its head again. "Can't unwrap it, not right now. So sad. Too full."

Willow nodded, then stood up straight and gathered her concentration together, pulling on the energies still left over from the spell she and the other Wiccans had performed to bring the Gnarl to them. "All right, then. How about a twin brother?" She pictured what she wanted to do, then raised both hands and *hurled* that thought straight into the demon's body.

The Gnarl gaped at her, then whined as its body began to first vibrate, then twist. It tried to rise, then fell back on all fours and howled as its form writhed and the skin of its back split open from its neck down to the base of its spine. A pair of thick, slick fingers pried the opening apart, then something dark and bloody-looking clawed its way to freedom and fell onto the dirt at the side of the demon. Willow waved her hand, and the nearly two-foot opening in the Gnarl's back welded itself shut, leaving only a thick, puckered scar as evidence of what had happened. The thing on the floor curled into a ball and began to grow as the original Gnarl panted and watched, too fascinated to be angry. It took less than sixty seconds before the demon was looking at a new version of itself, a not quite exact replica. The nifty thing about creating one from the other was that the creature already knew all the essential items on the do and the don't lists, was already bound by the same limitations and set of rules that had come from its birthing brother. All she had to do was task it.

The new Gnarl looked from her to its brother, then to Xander and Dawn on the floor. It backed away from them, as if it didn't want food that was already spoken for. "Hungry," it said simply.

Willow purposely avoided looking at the prone bodies of her former friends. Instead she made herself think of someone else and remember that the love of her life—or that part of her that Willow needed to bring her back—was being held captive.

"Good," she replied coldly. "I've ordered a couple of take-out meals to come to you. The first one ought to be getting here any minute."

Chapter Seven

"**O**h, thank God you're back!"

Giles had barely gotten through the door of the Magic Box before Anya was rushing toward him. "What's wrong?" he demanded. "Is someone injured?"

"No," Buffy said from over by the counter. She glanced worriedly at the clock. "At least, I don't think so."

"They're dead, Giles. I just know they are. They're hours late, and Werewolf Oz is still out rampaging somewhere." Anya was practically turning circles around him. "I even tried scrying for them and got a big fat *nothing* on the mystical map. That means they're probably dog food by now. Some werewolves are big on dismembering the bodies of their victims after they're dead. They—"

"I think that's quite enough," Giles interrupted her.

"Do I have permission to gag her?" Buffy asked.

Anya started to speak again and Giles had to hold up a hand to stop her full-speed babbling. "I take it Xander and Dawn are missing," he said. He directed his gaze at Buffy. "You've already tried her cell phone?"

"Yeah." Buffy looked frustrated. "I just keep getting her voice mail. I've left nine messages."

"I see." He looked from one to the other. "And we're absolutely certain they didn't just stop somewhere—the coffee shop, or the Bronze?"

"Xander and I had a date," Anya said loudly. When Buffy and Giles started at her, she flushed. "It was just for pizza and a video." She paused, then added a little wistfully, "And microwave popcorn."

Giles and Buffy turned to each other, then Buffy glanced at the clock again. She couldn't seem *not* to look at it, although right about now she was really wanting to strangle that weird little creature every time it made noise. What had Anya called it? A sprike. To her, it sounded like a cross between a bicycle part and something sharp. Couldn't she have just stuck with a bluebird?

"He's probably dead," Anya said again, but this time she sounded more mournful than panicked, almost resigned. "So's Dawn. Willow probably has some sort of spell on Oz in addition to making him stuck as a werewolf. His next three jobs are to probably fetch the rest of us."

"I rather think that's doubtful," Giles said.

"And Tara's ghost was crying," Buffy told him.

"We asked her what was wrong, but she wouldn't talk to us. Do you think she was crying just because she misses Willow? Or could she know something?"

Giles glanced around the loft, but the Ghost of Tara was nowhere to be seen. "No, I don't think so. Tara's spirit seems to be sort of a meter for all the Willow-related bad things going on." He rubbed his forehead. "I think it's much more likely that Willow has captured both Xander and Dawn, and will want to trade them for the Ghost of Tara."

Anya suddenly straighted. "I'll bet she's given in to her rage and has dumped some serious pain on them as revenge."

Buffy abandoned her post by the counter and began to pace. "What!"

Anya stepped into her path quickly enough to make Buffy stop short. "I think you'd better go over there," she told Buffy. "And get them back." She gestured vaguely at the shadows, knowing that somewhere in there was the Ghost of Tara. "What we have here is just spiritual. Sure, we could set Tara free, but there's nothing we can do to hurt her."

"Nor is there anything we *would* do," Giles added emphatically.

"If Willow does have Xander and Dawn, she could be wreaking major havoc. I don't think I have to remind you that humans are extremely fragile beings."

"I think we understand, Anya," Giles said hastily.

"I'm going over there," Buffy announced.

Anya rolled her eyes. "Finally!"

Giles touched Buffy's arm. "Buffy, you must be

very, *very* careful. Willow is extremely dangerous right now, and also unpredictable. I had no idea she would react as badly as she has to our imprisoning the Ghost of Tara. For her to walk away without even attempting to talk to Tara was utterly unthinkable."

Buffy looked at him impatiently. "And all of that's supposed to what—make me go stick my head in the sand like a camel?"

"Ostrich," Anya said helpfully.

"No, of course not," Giles said. "I just wanted to stress the danger."

"Stress and danger." Buffy shot him a wry look. "Now there's two words that have never been used in the same sentence."

He started to speak, and this time it was Buffy who held up her hand. "I'll be back as soon as I can, and hopefully with Xander and my sister."

"Be careful!" Giles called.

But the door had already closed behind her.

Buffy made her way to Willow's building via the quick and dirty; through people's yards, down alleys, over fences, and God help anything that tried to jump out at her and get in the way. She'd had enough of these games, and once she got Xander and Dawn back, she was going to sit down and have a long talk with Giles. Because really, what was the issue here? Willow's wickedness? Yeah, okay, so maybe she had done a big evil on Warren, but it wasn't like revisiting the crime scene was going to bring King Geek back to life. He was dead, kaput, less than charcoal. And while she couldn't justify Willow's actual killing of him, no matter how hard she tried, Buffy couldn't quite *not* justify it either.

See, it was all tied up in her mind, and in her heart of hearts—that place where no one but she could actually see. There was that dark part of her that said Warren had actually deserved what he got for killing Tara. And if she carried it on from there, remembering all the things that Willow had said about her and how it was all *her* fault that Tara had been killed because Warren had been going after Buffy, not Tara, she might even feel—

Better not go there.

Better to be *here* instead, on the sidewalk in front of Willow's building.

The sun was about to set, and there were enough clouds in the sky to paint everything a lovely shade of pink. It was so beautiful, it almost hurt to look at it: the kind of sunset that Willow and Tara might have shared together, walking hand in hand down to the Espresso Pump, or maybe she and Angel . . . now *there* was a ridiculous thought, since he'd fry the instant a couple of those pretty pink clouds separated and sent a sunbeam down on him. Willow had done an interesting job on her building, and when Buffy first arrived, the outside was dirty gray stone and metal, the same as everything else in the neighborhood. But the lower the sun sank in the west, the more Willow's chosen colors came out, gaining vibrancy with the darkness. Such spectacular shades of blue—had Willow picked these because they were restful, or because they matched the way she felt without her beloved Tara?

But Buffy couldn't dwell on those things now. She didn't have time to be soft, or to empathize with someone else's loss—even Willow's. She wanted her sister back, damn it, and Xander, too. And she was definitely going to make sure Willow knew it.

She gave it five more minutes and let the sun sink below the line of industrial buildings so that the shadows could lengthen, then she began circling the building.

Great. The door was gone.

Never mind that Buffy hadn't actually been able to get it *open* the last time she'd tried. Maybe it was an optical illusion, a camouflaging spell. On that theory, Buffy went tactile, running her hands over a surface that should have been corrugated tin, decaying wood, and rough stone, and feeling nothing but a metal so smooth and slick that it felt oily. She kept checking her hands—she couldn't help it—expecting to see residue, something thick and hideously messy like transmission fluid. But there was nothing. Her palms remained as clean and grease-free as the surface of the building stayed smooth. There wasn't a single seam or a hinge or *anything* to be found, and Buffy went over and around the surface, from ground level to as high as she could reach.

Zip.

Finally she went around to the back and got out the hook and the length of heavy nylon rope she'd brought along just for giggles and for door-deprived situations like this one. Standing in the shadows, she wound up and gave it a beautiful underhand toss. It sailed up and up and up—

—and instead of going over the edge, it bounced against something Buffy couldn't see, and thunked back down to the sidewalk.

So she tried again. And again. Higher and higher, and something like fourteen tries later, Buffy finally admitted defeat. Willow had thought of everything: invisible doors and windows, unseen walls that rose much higher above the roofline than Buffy could ever hope to throw. Like it or not, there was no way she was getting into that loft.

She had about five seconds of resigned defeat, then the anger hit her. "Damn it, Willow, you come down here and talk to me!" she yelled as loud as she could. "I know you're not a coward, so stop acting like one!"

Buffy waited, hoping her nasty little insult would get Willow's hackles up.

Nada.

"Come on, Will—let's talk about this. I know you've got Xander and Dawn up there. Let them come down and we can work this out."

Let them come down? Buffy spun on the sidewalk in frustration, feeling like she'd watched way too many movies. Here she was, acting like some badass hostage negotiator when Willow was the one who held all the cards, not to mention the actual whiz bang power. Time and time again, it had become painfully—literally—obvious that Buffy's Slayerness was not going to be enough to pull them out of the fire with Willow, and now she was afraid someone had turned the oven knob to *broil*. For crying out loud, she couldn't even be sure Willow was actually inside.

Finally, rather than stand outside and risk making a fool of herself—or worse, plead—Buffy gave up and headed back to the Magic Box.

Chapter Eight

"**H**umph," Willow said out loud. "The Buffy I used to know wouldn't have given up so easily." She watched Buffy disappear down the street, then turned away from the window. Of course, the Buffy she used to know hadn't had to face someone as powerful as Willow. That had to really be frosting her, considering Willow had played sidekick all those years, second fiddle to the main attraction. Now Willow wasn't just the star, she was the *producer* of this little Sunnydale hit parade.

What had Buffy said? *"Let them come down and we can work this out."* Right. As far as Willow was concerned, there was only one thing to work out: the release of the Ghost of Tara. And until Buffy and her little band of minions made that happen, Willow would whittle them down to nothing.

• • •

If I'm not real, then why do things like this keep happening to me?

Dawn stared up at the cave's ceiling. It looked like a long way up, but in reality it probably wasn't all that much taller than the height of a man—right now, everything looked bigger. It was a side effect of lying flat on your back in the dirt and being unable to move. She was pretty sure she was crying because her vision kept wavering and blurring, like a car windshield in the rain when the wipers weren't working fast enough. But even that was a guess, because she couldn't feel any of the tears that might be slipping down her face.

She had tried talking to Xander, but finally gave up. Every now and then she could hear him trying to tell the demon to go away, to not do the munch-mouth thing on whatever part of him it had focused on. As for herself, after the first three or four strips of flesh had been peeled from her chest—she could tell that was the target area by really, really straining her eyes downward—she'd decided just to close her eyes each time the demon approached her with its wide and hungry leer. It was actually a sort of denial: She couldn't feel it, and she couldn't see it, so therefore it must not be happening. This line of thinking was very high on the hot list when the alternative was having a demon eat you alive. It was also very helpful during the times that the creature would swing pieces of flesh into her point of view and tell her that this particular tidbit came from her friend, and wasn't she glad it was he instead of she?

Now and then Dawn would wonder if this was what insects caught in a spiderweb went through: the entrapment; the paralyzing sting of the predator's bite or jab; the eventual, horrifying digestion.

There'd been a bump on the head involved, and she'd woken up with one heck of a headache that wasn't helped by discovering that her hands and ankles were duct taped and she'd been thrown over someone's shoulder like a side of beef. The generous scream in her throat got nowhere—it, too, was stopped by the unpleasantly sticky side of the strip of silver tape across her mouth. Her eyes were open—thank God they hadn't taped those shut too—but she couldn't tell where they'd taken her, other than it was dark, damp, and smelled nasty, all of which added up to "tomb."

One glimpse—that's all she'd had of Xander's wide-eyed face as she was swung down and dropped painfully onto the ground. The face of her abductor came into view, some grubby-looking alley creep who looked far too well fed and dressed to be homeless. He grinned down at her, and Dawn wanted to gag at the mouth full of missing and rotting teeth. If he bit her, she was going to need a tetanus shot.

What she hadn't known at the time was that something far, *far* worse was going to do just that.

Her kidnapper said something she couldn't hear, and someone outside Dawn's field of vision grunted something in return. Then he shuffled away, disappearing into a darkened doorway around which a bunch of pentagrams had been engraved. Great—now she was being wrapped and delivered like something off the shelf at Anya's shop. She just hoped Buffy would get here in time before they put her in a circus, or did something worse—such as cook her to a powder and sell her in little pouches, like animal poachers did to the rarest of the rare species.

But . . . Buffy *didn't* get there in time.

Dawn didn't know what kind of creature this was, but it sure appeared to be having a lot of fun. Her head throbbed, and dirt and rocks were digging into her back, but all that went away after the demon held up its forefinger, which was tipped by a vicious-looking fingernail that appeared to be dripping. With a rapturous expression, it had given her a long and excruciating scratch along her exposed forearm, and then everything had gone numb after that.

Which was, Dawn thought, a damned good thing, because according to this beast's raspy, singsong voice, his entire purpose on this earth was specifically to "unwrap" her. Could a person's ears get paralyzed as well? She almost wished hers had, because at least then she wouldn't have to listen to the horrible little singing poems the demon kept making up. All that was hard enough to ignore, but the worst horror came when it kept holding up the thin strips of her flesh that it was apparently peeling off her body with its fingernails; it seemed to take great pleasure in dangling them in front of her face before slurping them down like disgusting strands of pinkish pasta. Capping off the entire hellish experience was the way it would switch from chewing to lapping at the blood that must be dribbling from her wounds. Dawn could tell that was what it was doing, because it only took a couple of times for the demon's chin to end up coated in blood. *Her* blood.

She'd spent so much time denying the truth of that terrible day when she'd found out that she was supposedly nothing but a sparkle of energy, a key to be used by someone else to access a source of power or open the door to another universe, that her own thoughts made her feel like a traitor now.

Yet all she could think was, *Please God, let this not be happening. Let this not be real.* . . .

"I'm going out," Anya told Giles. "I just can't wait here any longer wondering if Xander's safe or a hundred and eighty pounds of werewolf chow."

Giles looked up at her, concern etched across his features. "I wouldn't recommend that, Anya. Even as a vengeance demon, I don't know that you would be protected against a werewolf's scratch or bite. You'd be taking a terrible risk."

"Well, I do have *some* advantage over a mere mortal like you," she said smartly. "Three times the strength and the teleportation thing, remember? If worse comes to worse, I'll just pop out of tooth range."

"Since arguing is obviously not doing any good here," Giles said as he went over to the weapons cabinet and pulled open the doors, "I suppose the best I can do is remind you to take the tranquilizer gun."

Anya sighed and took the weapon. "For being not much more than a dog on supernatural steroids, Oz certainly is a lot of trouble."

"Just be careful," Giles told her. "I'd much prefer you'd stay here until Buffy returns."

Anya rolled her eyes. "Please. Do you really think

Buffy's going to come back with some good news? She's more likely to come back with a couple of black eyes and a broken arm."

Giles started to reply, but she spun on her heel and headed out, leaving him to think long and hard about what she'd said.

"Great," Anya muttered to herself. "Once again, here I am, wandering around in the dark and carrying an annoyingly heavy weapon when I should be turning unfaithful men into fish food and throwing them into piranha-filled rivers."

She pressed her lips together and scanned the street, one of countless little side avenues in Sunnydale. The little pools of light cast by the streetlamps weren't much help in cutting through the early spring darkness. Although she and the others hadn't thought much about it, there was always one holiday or another coming up; had she still been human and married to Xander like she was supposed to have been, she might have tried her hand at a big ham dinner with all the trimmings in defiance of the upcoming big bunny day, although it still puzzled her why humans cooked pork instead of rabbit when so much of the season's retail market was devoted to the Easter Bunny.

But she wasn't married, and she wasn't human anymore. She wasn't going to walk down the aisle— face it, even if she and Xander ever got back together, she'd *never* trust him about *that* again—and she certainly wasn't going to cook a meal where she'd face a kitchen-load of dirty dishes afterward.

Anya looked up and frowned. She'd been wandering around for at least an hour, and though she knew more or less where she was within the maze that was Sunnydale's residential area, she really had no idea where she *should* go. The mall seemed like a bad idea, even though she hoped that's where Dawn would ultimately turn up. Teenagers were always testing the limits of authority, and this one was no different. Xander was another matter. He wou—

Anya froze.

What was that shadow, the one just below the bushes to the side of the house she was passing right now? Were her eyes playing tricks on her, or was it *moving*? Anya forced her feet to get moving again, as if nothing in the world could bother her and she wasn't being stalked by a werewolf that probably outweighed her by a hundred pounds. Her first instinct, of course, was to teleport out of there, but what good would that do? She'd be safe—which was actually a whole *lot* of good—but Oz would still be wandering around and munching at will, and there would still be the unresolved issue of Xander's and Dawn's disappearance. She *did* have a tranquilizer gun, and she knew for a fact that it had worked quite well in the past . . . provided she didn't miss and send a load of sleepy-time into the nearest tree trunk.

More rustling, but stealthy in that keeping-pace-with-her kind of way that always freaked out the busty blondes in the horror movies. Anya could definitely appreciate the fright factor—hers was climbing with each house that she passed. But there was light ahead, a welcome square of it, and as Anya got closer, she didn't know whether to sneer or to be grateful over just how far the human male would go to get a good steak. In the next driveway over, beneath the glow of an outside yard light, some guy and his wife were wearing heavy jackets and standing outside, hovering over a couple of hunks of beef on a Weber grill.

Her unseen stalker was still there, and she was maybe forty feet away from the rather questionable safety of other people when a man sidled into step next to her.

She stopped and turned to frown at him—she'd long ago lost her fear of strange men (she'd found them to be excellent objects upon which to hone her verbal skills)—then realized that he wasn't a man at all. "Oh, go away," she said in exasperation. "You're a vampire, I'm a vengeance demon. It's really a bad mix."

Still in his human form, the guy looked at her and grinned. He was really very nice looking, with light brown hair and brown eyes, a very all-American type. He was even wearing a cap—Chicago Cubs—and a denim jacket to complete the picture. Anyone else would have probably been fooled, but most of these creatures hardly ever bothered to brush their teeth, and Anya could smell the blood from his last meal coming out of his mouth. In fact it hadn't even been that long since he'd eaten.

"Afraid I can't do that, Anya."

Her frown deepened as she stared at him. He had an Australian accent—how interesting considering his baseball-and-apple-pie outfit. He was still utterly unfamiliar—a tourist, perhaps. "Have we met?"

He laughed. "An experienced vengeance demon like yourself, I would've thought you could come up with a better line than that."

"I'm not trying to pick you up, idiot," she snapped. "How did you know my name?" Something was wrong here, so she decided to keep walking. She'd taken maybe five more steps toward that now very enticingly lit driveway when she couldn't go any farther because there was someone else, a second vampire, standing in her way.

"The same way I do," the new one said. "We all do."

All?

With an unpleasant start, Anya realized that there were now *three* vampires around her, all of whom looked and dressed very much alike. The second one had that same Down Under accent; maybe they were brothers. But that still didn't explain how they knew who she was when she'd never seen them before. "All right," she said. "You stumped me. What gives?"

The third one tapped the rim of his cap respectfully. "We were just passing through, mum. Going to Los Angeles. We've 'eard a vampire can make a fair livin' out there, providin' 'e can stay away from that Angel fella."

"Well boys, feel free to keep on going," Anya said. "In case you haven't noticed, we're already a bit overloaded on the undead around here."

"So we've been told," said the second one. "But

that's really not our concern. We're just out to make a little bit o' wages on the way."

Anya raised an eyebrow. "Is that what this is? A tacky little sidewalk robbery?"

The first one actually looked insulted. "Of course not. We're honest, 'ard-working men."

At Anya's baffled expression, the third vamp finally shed some light on the situation. "You've got a fair price on your pretty head."

Anya's eyes widened. "A price? You mean like a bounty?"

The first one nodded vigorously. "Exactly."

"Who—" Anya stopped. "Never mind. I think I know."

"Dark witch," one of them told her. "Be a right attractive lady if she'd lose that black lipstick."

Willow—of course. That must be what had happened to Xander and Dawn: Obviously Willow was holding them prisoner and was going to demand the Ghost of Tara as a trade. At least they hadn't been eaten alive or clawed by Oz. She'd just let these Aussies take her right to them, and once she knew where they were being held, she'd teleport away and tell Buffy and Giles. Piece of cake.

But first, she had a question. "How much is the bounty?" she demanded.

The top guy gave a falsely careless shrug. "Hundred apiece. Right on the line for a bus ticket each."

Anya's mouth worked. "Three hundred dollars—is that *all*?" She shook a finger at him. "I'm worth much more than that, you know. I once had a man offer to pay me my weight in gold not to turn him into a termite."

"Really." The second vampire looked impressed. "I imagine you ended up a right rich lady."

Anya raised one eyebrow as a faint smile of remembrance crossed her mouth. "It was really fun to watch when the anteater got him." The vampire winced, but Anya waved away any more comments and started walking again. "Anyway, it's a deal—lead on. I was actually looking to talk to her, anyway." The vampires eyed one another doubtfully, then obediently fell into step around her.

"Bit of a surprise that you'd be so cooperative and all," commented the first one, who appeared to be the leader. "Bein' as . . ." He didn't finish.

"What?" Anya demanded. They were just about up to the driveway where the couple was having their ridiculous November barbecue. "I really have no patience for riddles. Spit it out."

"If you're going t' open your blasted mouth about it," snapped the second Aussie, "you'd better well dose her with the witch's poison first."

Poison? Anya halted hard enough to send the vampire behind her stumbling into her back. She pushed him away, hard, then began a slow, self-protective spin in the middle of the trio, trying to keep her eye on all of them at once. "Hold it," she said. "When did poison come into this?"

The leading vamp pulled out an elongated wooden stick, very thin, with a very sharp point. He held it up for her to look at. "Your witchy pal's got plans for you, just like the others."

This good situation was going rapidly downhill. "What plans?"

"Well, that explains why she's so willin' to come along," said the second guy. "She 'as no idea what's waitin' for her."

"What 'plans'?" Anya demanded loudly. Out of the far corner of her eye, she saw Mr. BBQ look up from his grill and turn his attention in their direction. He wasn't far away—no more than thirty feet or so.

The leader lifted his toothpick-shaped stick higher. "This stuff 'ere is from the fingernail of a demon she's got all hidden away," he explained, looking almost sympathetic. "It'll make things a lot easier. You won't feel a thing when he . . . well, does what he does to you."

Anya felt the blood drain from her face. "Wait—demon? What kind of demon?"

"Don't know specifics," offered the third vampire. "But it sure is a nasty way to go, havin' the skin peeled right off of you while you watch the creature eat it and drink what's dribblin' out." He shuddered and shook his head. "Can't run, can't scream—but at least you can't feel it, either."

"Oh no," Anya said. Xander and Dawn were being eaten alive? Wait—she couldn't think about that right now. She had to stay focused on these three or she'd end up joining the dinner buffet. She back-stepped and found one of the vampires right behind her, using his body as a wall. She twisted to the side and barely jerked away from the grab he made at her wrist.

The leader held out his thin stick-thing again.

"Come on, mum. This'll make the 'ole experience bearable." He followed his words with a jab at her arm, but Anya eluded it.

The second one tried to snatch at her, and she swatted his hand aside, then yanked out the tranquilizer gun and held it in front of her. The Aussie boys eyed it cautiously, but she wasn't fool enough to think they were truly afraid of it. Unless it was loaded with wooden stakes, it wasn't going to do much harm . . . or so they thought. The tranquilizer dart inside *would* knock one of them out, but then she'd have to reload. By then, they'd be all over her. She could teleport out of there, but that would end her chance of pounding on one of these dweebs until she found out exactly where Xander and Dawn were being held. The way she saw it, the big problem here wasn't so much the vampires, it was that poison business.

"Lady, are these guys giving you a hard time?" demanded a masculine voice. "My name's Murphy, and I'm head of the neighborhood-watch program on this street. We don't put up with stuff like that around here, so you fellows just better move along."

The two vampires in front of her spun and found themselves face-to-face with the winter barbecue guy. He hadn't come over empty-handed, either: Though he wasn't making a big show of it, the man had a long, double-pronged cooking fork he held confidently in his right hand. "Sod off," snarled one.

"Mind your own business!" snapped another.

What a great diversion. "Yes," Anya said loudly. "They are. So I'd be very grateful if you would stick your fork in their hearts so I can go on my way."

For an astonished moment, no one said anything as BBQ man gaped at her while the other three froze. When Murphy's gaze settled on the tranquilizer gun still clutched in one hand, Anya decided this was the perfect time to take the offensive; she still wasn't willing to run, but she was always up for a good fight now that the odds were a little more even. A neat, tight spin sent a sturdy sidekick right into the gut of the bloodsucker who kept hovering behind her. Mr. BBQ's mouth dropped open even farther, then the leader snarled and swiped at Anya again with that aggravating poison-tipped stick of his. He missed—barely—and Anya punched him solidly on the left side of his jaw. The last guy made a two-fisted grab for her, and *finally* Murphy decided to spring into action. He jabbed out with his fork, and the pointed ends of it sank nicely into the right arm of Anya's latest attacker.

"Arrrrrgh!" Those boyish good looks disappeared instantly, and then he was all vampire. Murphy's mouth worked soundlessly, and he yanked the fork free, then backed away; before Anya could react, the vampire drew back and hit BBQ Man hard enough to knock him out and send his unconscious form sliding so far, he ended up right back in his own driveway.

The woman who'd been out there with him—presumably, his wife—screamed and rushed over to him, then began shrieking at the top of her lungs: *"Call the cops! Call the cops! My husband's being attacked!"* Her voice had the unsettling ability to echo up and down the deserted streets, and apparently

Murphy hadn't been kidding about that neighborhood-watch thing; lights instantly began popping on in windows all around them.

Now all three of the Aussies had slid into vampire-face, so Anya let herself morph to vengeance-demon mode. She'd be stronger that way, faster—

"Oh no, you don't."

She gasped as hands closed around both arms and lifted her off her feet. Before she could *think* about teleporting, the deadly tip of the toothpick-stick was there, headed right for her cheek—

Then something horribly loud and wet sounding snarled viciously from the darkness only a few feet away, and all hell really *did* break loose.

Chapter Nine

"Very nice, very good, you have brought me tasty food."

Giles's eyesight was now limited to only what ran across his field of vision, but there was certainly nothing wrong with his hearing. Still, that wasn't much help—he understood the words, but couldn't identify the source.

He wondered if his car was still parked out by the cemetery gate. It wasn't such an absurd thing to think about right now, because the best he could hope for seemed to be that Buffy or Anya would find it and then hunt until they found him, too. It had really been quite foolish of him not to notice that he was being followed when he'd come out of the specialty foods store—the only place he could get his preferred brand of English tea and real, honest-to-God cranberry scones—and had gotten into his car. It was such a small thing, but he'd wanted that tea because it brought him more comfort and mental clarity than anything, and he certainly felt that, given the circumstances, he could use that right now. In fact, that same mental clarity might have prevented his idiocy in not disabling the function on his key lock—newfangled thing—that automatically unlocked *every* door in the car instead of just the driver's side when he pressed the button.

The creepy little demon that had carjacked him had reminded him very much of a demon named Skyler, whom Faith had murdered years ago. Giles hadn't seen one in years, and this one hadn't identified himself as he'd pressed the point of a wicked-looking dagger into Giles's right side, pushing on it until the exceedingly sharp point had penetrated his coat and drawn blood from the soft tissue beneath it. There was no chance of grabbing the sword with that much invested: The dagger's hilt was rimmed with sharpened decorative points, and all that was reachable was a deadly, two-sided blade, and there was no room to maneuver within the car. The ironic thing was that Faith had used a very similar knife to kill a very similar demon.

"You'll go where I tell you," the demon had rasped. "If you give me trouble, I'll deliver you in pieces. Makes no difference to me."

"Where are we—*ow!*"

"Shut up!"

So much for any kind of information flow. He'd

had hopes that he'd find out more when they got to where they were headed—the most disused and the oldest of the cemeteries in Sunnydale—but that notion had been quickly crushed. He'd driven as the demon had instructed him, then pulled up and cut the lights and the engine. No sooner had he turned the key to off than something sharp had pricked him on the back of his right hand, and that was it. No movement, no feeling . . . *nothing.* It was terrifyingly familiar, except this time it was worse, because it encompassed nearly *everything:* legs, arms, face—even his lips. The only things that seemed to work were his eyes and his tongue, and neither was very efficient given his inability to move his head or lips. An eyesight-jarring trip through the darkness while tossed over the demon's shoulder like a wounded soldier, a descent down a flight of dark and dirt-encrusted steps, and he'd been rudely dropped to the ground and left there in a pile of jumbled limbs. His abductor hadn't even had the courtesy to tell Giles where they were or why he was here.

And so here he was, presumably lying on the ground in a cave—he could think of nothing else that had a dirt-and-rock structure like what was available from his severely restricted viewpoint. The lighting, obviously torchlight, flickered in and out, and there were enough occasional shadows moving around him that he was confident someone—or *something*—else was here. When he finally heard that high-pitched, singsong voice, Giles had the sinking feeling he was seriously going to regret finding out.

"Very nice, very good, you have brought me tasty food."

Oh, dear.

There was a lot of screaming, and a lot of blood, but that didn't last long—even with three of them, the young Aussies were simply no match for the blood-thirsty werewolf they'd never expected to encounter. No one had silver, not even Anya, and certainly not in any fashion that might have been used as a weapon against this oversize, snarling beast. Anya still wasn't sure if she was immune to the effects of a werewolf's bite or scratch, so she threw herself out of the fray, then rushed toward Mr. BBQ and his wife, intent on getting them into their house and out of wolf's notice.

"Call the cops! Get the neighborhood waaaatch!" Mrs. Murphy was still screaming, except now she was trying to pull her husband's unconscious body toward the open door of the garage. The steaks were still on the grill, and they smelled pretty good even though they were getting seriously overcooked. A shame to waste good beef like that.

"Oh, for God's sake, would you be *quiet*!" Anya snapped. Mrs. Murphy eyes bulged, and her thankfully silent mouth hung open, then Anya realized she was still in demon mode. "Oops—sorry." Of course, changing back to human form didn't help. At this point, all it did was shock the frightened woman even more. "You know what? Just deal with it." She shoved the woman aside, then grabbed Mr. BBQ by his wrists and pulled as hard as she could. He was surprisingly heavy—a lot of muscle under that plaid hunter's jacket, which was probably what made him feel brave enough to face off with three strangers on the street. Too bad his supernatural experience was limited to none when he decided to be a hero.

"Come on, lady," Anya commanded. "Help me get him inside now." The Murphy woman was still stunned enough to be doing the head-bob thing between Anya and the carnage going on not so far away down the sidewalk. "Tonight, please!" Anya yelled at her, and suddenly Mrs. BBQ snapped out of it and, after one last look over at Oz, began pulling in earnest on her husband's arm. Together, they managed to get him far enough inside the garage so that the door could close. "There," Anya said with satisfaction. "You just close up and stay inside for a while, and everything will be fine. Oh—don't bother with the cops. Those guys out there will be dust by the time they arrive."

Anya turned to leave, and the woman grabbed her by the sleeve. "But what about you, miss? That thing out there . . ." Her voice faded away, and Anya had to be privately amazed at the adaptability of the human psyche. Anya looked normal *now*, so therefore she must be. Mrs. Murphy had convinced herself that surely anything other than that had been nothing but the stress and panic of the moment working on her. Anya didn't have the heart—or the time—to scare her just for the fun of it. She had to get back out there and zap Fuzzy Oz with the tranquilizer gun before he loped away. And if she hurried, she might even be able to get one of those vamps while he could still be persuaded to talk. Maybe.

"I'll be fine," she said cheerfully. She stepped out and left the woman with her husband in their garage. "Here," she offered, grabbing the handle of the double garage door. "I'll close the door for you." One hard pull and there was a handy wall of painted sheet metal between her and the BBQ neighborhood-watch couple.

Running as fast as she could, Anya headed back down the driveway. The three vamps were still there, but they were going down fast. Alas, Anya had no sympathy for them other than to find out if anyone knew where Xander and Dawn were being held prisoner. She made it a third of the way down the drive when the Oz-wolf literally ripped the head off one vampire. No head, no vampire, and he went down in a puddle of decapitated dust.

"Oz, wait!" she cried, stretching her speed to the limit. "Don't kill them all! They're useful!" Great—here she was shouting at a werewolf as though it could understand her. Oddly enough, the werewolf actually seemed to hesitate . . . and for its trouble, got whacked on the side of the head. It spun in a rage and swiped at the bloodsucker who'd hit it. Despite his visible injuries, the second Aussie somehow managed to lean out of range, then grinned as his brother raised the poison-tipped piece of wood and jabbed it downward at the werewolf's back.

Anya snatched the extra-long stick out of the vampire's grip before it could graze the Oz-wolf's back. Still in its downward arc, the bloodsucker's fist thunked uselessly against Oz's fur-covered shoulder blade. "Oh no, you don't!" The leader bared his teeth at her, then his face went blank with surprise as Anya drove the skinny piece of wood right smack through the center of his chest. "There," she said with satisfaction. "Couldn't have wished it better myself. Bye-bye."

There was no time to appreciate the fine sifting of Australian dust on the evening's breeze. When Anya looked up, the werewolf had the last vampire in its heavily clawed grip, and its teeth were fast descending on the screaming bloodsucker's head. "Oz, *no!*"

Drat.

So then it was just she and the Oz-wolf. She had a two-, maybe three-second reprieve as the werewolf drew back his head and sneezed vampire dust out of its nose. Then it turned its head and its bloodshot gaze caught hers. The beast's muzzle was heavy with gore, and Anya really didn't want to have that meaty-smelling mouth anywhere close to her throat.

"Nice Oz," she said. "Nice doggie. Nice, nice, nice." It was all she could think of to say as she backed away and fumbled to get the tranquilizer gun up and aimed in the right direction. Well, sort of—she'd really planned on firing the thing from a considerable distance away, and with the Oz-wolf only about five feet from her, her hands were shaking rather badly. The werewolf reared up and faced her, then just stood there, looking from her to the gun and back at her. It was the strangest thing she'd ever seen a werewolf do—not that she'd seen a lot of werewolves, but strange, nonetheless.

Anya fired.

The tranquilizer dart sank into the werewolf's left shoulder, but the creature didn't give it a chance to settle. A lightning-fast grab and it yanked the dart free and threw it . . . at her feet. Anya gasped and figured she was dead; she should have known better. This wasn't just any old werewolf; it was Oz, and he was easily the brainiest guy she'd ever met. Why wouldn't he, then, end up being the brainiest werewolf she'd ever met too?

Luckily the tranquilizer appeared to be taking effect. The Oz-wolf staggered a bit, then went down on one knee in front of her. Anya was too amazed to run, and too curious—possibly for her own good—to reload the tranq gun. The next five seconds, which could easily fall into that mythical "longest of her life" category, passed, and then Oz's fur and flesh began to writhe and twist over itself; the fur pulled in as his body reabsorbed it, the jaw retracted, and his teeth sunk back into bone. Anya watched the fantastic transformation until kneeling in front of her was a blood-soaked and very naked Oz.

"Oz?" Stupid question. Of course it was Oz . . . and other parts of him that she really had no right or reason to be viewing. Anya cast a quick glance behind her, then yanked off her jacket and tossed it over his shoulder. "Oz, can you hear me?"

"Anya . . . sorry, didn't mean to scare you."

"I'd rather hear you say that than 'didn't mean to kill you.'" Another glance around told her that, with the quieting of the battle, people were starting to get brave enough to open their doors. No doubt Mrs. BBQ had called the cops, anyway, and they'd be there any minute. "We have to get out of here."

She tugged his arm, and the good part was that he stood quite well considering he'd been doing the four-footed walk for some time. The bad part was that he went right back down to his knees. "Tranquilizer . . . ," he said faintly.

"Oh no, you can't take a nap now!" She pulled on him again, determined to get him up.

Oz's hair was plastered against his sweating forehead, and his green eyes fluttered. "Not much strength left," he managed. "Took everything I had to break Willow's spell."

His eyes started to roll back in his head, and Anya slapped him . . . but not too hard. It could be dangerous to make a werewolf angry, even one that didn't want to be a werewolf. "Wake up," she insisted. "We *can't* stay here. There are people coming, the police. How will you explain your nakedness to them?"

That seemed to do the trick—at least enough of it to make him want to try. She got him to his feet, and he shivered as he let the jacket slide down around his waist, then he struggled to tie the arms at one hip. He looked like a skinny version of an urban Tarzan. Well, except for the disgustingly bloody mouth.

As though he could read her thoughts, Oz turned his head and spat into the grass. "Gross."

"Definitely," she agreed. "Hang on, wolf-boy. We've got toothpaste at the Magic Box!"

Chapter Ten

Buffy was standing in front of the counter at the Magic Box and wondering where the heck everyone was when Anya nearly dragged a naked Oz through the front door.

"Buffy, a little help!" Anya gasped. She was just about tapped out—even with her hidden demon strength. Dragging Oz halfway across town while trying to keep him out of the curious line of sight of people on the street had sapped her of nearly every ounce of her energy.

Buffy didn't need to be told twice, and together they got Oz propped on a chair in front of the table, where he promptly put his head on his arms and passed out. He was filthy and scratched up, covered in dead, crushed leaves and mud, not to mention the dried blood caked all over his hands and across his face.

Anya and Buffy stared at him for a long moment, then Anya went to a closet and came back with a blanket to drape across his back.

"Is he . . . *safe*?" Buffy asked warily. "He's not gonna suddenly bounce back to wolf-boy and use us for chew-toys, is he?"

"I don't think so," Anya said. She ran a shaky hand across her forehead, then grimaced when she saw her dirty fingernails. "I mean I don't *think* he's going to change back," she added. "After he killed all the vampires, he mumbled something to me about it being really difficult to break Willow's spell."

Buffy chewed her lip. "All right. He did come back from the Far East able to master his body and keep from changing, even during the full moon." She paused, then had to amend that. "At least until he got really jealous of Tara."

"Love will screw you up every time," Anya said a little caustically. "I have to wash my hands."

Buffy followed her to the small bathroom and watched as Anya ran the water and squeezed lemon-smelling soap into her palm. "What was that you said back there about Oz killing all the vampires? What vampires?"

Anya nodded. "There were three of them. They surrounded me and said there was a bounty on my head and that they were going to earn money by taking me to Willow. I figured that was a good thing, because it seemed obvious that's where Xander and Dawn were." Anya rinsed her hands, watched the dirty water swirl down the drain, and frowned at the memory.

"Except then he pulled out this poison-tipped piece of wood and tried to poke me with it." She grabbed a hand towel. "That's when he started talking about the flesh-eating and blood-drinking demon that's eating Xander and Dawn alive."

Buffy had been silent until now, but this last bit of news made her jerk. "What?!"

Anya nodded again. "That's also when the BBQ man poked the leader with his fork and we all started fighting and Oz jumped out of the bushes and saved my life. It was a very harrowing experience."

Buffy gripped the edge of the sink. "Are you serious? Willow gave my sister and Xander to a creature that's eating them?"

"Alive."

Buffy's mouth dropped open, then she closed it hard enough to make her teeth ache. "Where are they?"

Anya stepped around her to get out of the bathroom, and Buffy followed her back over to the table. Oz was still dead to the world, and Anya looked at him and sighed. "I don't know. Unfortunately, Oz wasn't quite himself yet, and he ate the last vampire before I could get the answer to that question."

Buffy's fists balled at her sides in frustration. "So we have no idea?"

"Right."

"They could be anywhere."

"Right."

Buffy spun. "We need to talk to Giles. There can't be *that* many places in Sunnydale where you can hide a flesh-eating demon and . . . and"—she gritted her teeth—"and *feed* it. He'll be able to help us figure this out."

"Good idea," Anya agreed. "Where is he?"

They looked at each other, then at the empty Magic Box, and neither one had any idea.

They'd only been sitting there for a few indecisive minutes, holding a cautious vigil over Oz, when someone knocked on the door of the Magic Box.

Buffy and Anya looked at each other, then Buffy's expression darkened. She could think of only one person who would have to knock—

Willow.

She was at the door and yanking it open before even thinking about the possible consequences. In fact, who *cared* about that. Willow had taken her baby sister and had fed her to some atrocious, skin-munching monster, and she was going to pummel her three times for every bite that had been taken out of Dawn, every single toothmark—

But it wasn't Willow waiting outside.

Instead, it was some skanky, mean-faced little demon with deep-set eyes and elflike ears, a pair of the standard pointy horns coming out each side of his forehead. There was lots of long facial hair going on, and, of course, the usual sharp teeth that looked like they hadn't been brushed in a couple of hundred years.

"What do you want?" Buffy snapped. Her patience was at an all-time low, her stress over the edge of high. "You'd better have a good reason to be standing here or I'm going to put you face-first into the concrete."

But the demon, who looked the same kind as that weasel-like guy who'd once tried to sell Mayor Wilkins's *Books of Ascension,* seemed anything but troubled by her sharpness. That other one—Buffy remembered his name was Skyler—had been a sniveling little coward, but this one didn't appear the least bit concerned or afraid. "I'm just the messenger," he said flatly. "You wanna hear the message or not? If you punch me or something, I ain't talking."

"Fine," Buffy said, and yanked him inside the store. "Spill it."

He stumbled inside and scowled at her, then reached inside his pants pocket and pulled out a folded piece of paper. "Here," he said. "I'm supposed to take an answer back." The demon looked disgusted. "I really hate this," he complained. "I gotta find another line of work. Maybe I'll take a home-study course and become an accountant. That way I can work at home in my pajamas and no one has to know I'm a demon."

"We're really not interested in your job aptitude," Anya said as Buffy snatched the note out of his hand.

"It's from Willow," Buffy said.

"Big surprise." Anya stepped closer so she could read over Buffy's shoulder.

"It says she'll trade the Ghost of Tara for the release of Xander, Dawn, and"—Buffy looked up, confirming their most recent fear—"Giles."

Anya's face paled. "God, Buffy—would Willow turn all three of them over to a disgusting flesh-eating demon?"

"Hey, those guys are Gnarls," snapped the little

demon standing in front of them. "I don't eat humans, so don't go lumping all of us together." He glared at Anya. "You, specifically, ought to know better."

"Shut up," Buffy said before Anya could reply. "I'm pretty sure if I kill you, Willow will send someone else." There was something in the tone of her voice that made the demon decide not to argue. She crumpled up Willow's note. "She wants us to bring the Ghost of Tara to her and she'll let everyone go. Tell her it's fine by me," Buffy said. "Just tell us where. She—"

"Has to send Giles back here first," Anya interrupted.

Buffy turned to stare at her. "What? Why?"

"Because only Giles can release the boundary spell," Anya reminded her. "Without him, we can't get the Ghost of Tara out of this building, and he has to be *here,* in the Magic Box, to say the incantation to break it." She inclined her head toward the demon. "Whether she likes it or not, Willow has to let Giles go before she gets Tara."

"And then she has to hold up her end of the bargain and release Xander and Dawn," Buffy added. "That's a nonnegotiable point." Her expression was almost dangerous. "And they'd *better* be okay."

The demon looked decidedly unhappy. "She's not gonna like this. She really hates . . . what did she call it? I remember: *limitations.* I'm pretty sure she was expecting a simple yes."

"Giles told her about the spell's requirements the last time she came by," Anya said. "It's not our fault she's doing the convenient no-short-term-memory thing."

Buffy sent the pointy-eared demon a blackly humorous smile. "Remember, you're just the messenger."

"We used to behead them all the time in the Middle Ages," Anya said helpfully. "Maybe Willow won't be so hard. she'll probably only cut out your tongue."

The demon had lost most of his self-confident air. Now he swallowed. "Great."

"Of course," Anya continued, "if you don't come back at all, she'll probably send a demon-seeking fireball to consume you."

"I think your welcome just wore out," Buffy said, and gave him a not so gentle push toward the front door. "Go tell Willow we're waiting."

The demon pulled open the door, and this time he actually looked a little woeful. "Great," he said again. "I—"

"End of conversation," Buffy snapped, and shoved him out the door. She closed it before he had the chance to come back and whine some more. She turned back to Anya and took a deep breath. "How badly are they going to be hurt?"

Anya folded her arms and hugged herself. "I'm not sure," she admitted. "Those vampires—they were pretty specific about what was being done to Xander and Dawn, but then, how much can you really trust a vampire?" She blinked, then amended: "At least, an evil one."

"We're all evil."

Both Buffy and Anya jumped at the sound of Spike's voice. They'd all but forgotten the vampire who, since Buffy had pulled his scorching self out of the sun-light, had apparently decided that all he wanted to do was huddle in the darkest corner of the shop. Now, even though he wasn't looking at either of them, he was nodding to himself. "Oh, sure—you can see it, in here." He thumped his chest. "Evil, evil, evil. Dirty and bloody and not to be trusted." He lifted his head and squinted across the room at Buffy. "Don't trust them!" he suddenly cried. "They'll kill you and suck out your self!"

Buffy swallowed, trying to ignore him. "Willow wouldn't hurt them that badly." She hesitated, and Spike seemed to pull back in on himself, sitting on the floor against the wall with his knees drawn up and his head resting on his crossed arms. Finally she had to ask. "Would she?"

"The Willow you once knew is being driven further and further away."

Buffy sucked in a breath at the sound of the Ghost of Tara's voice whispering in one ear. "I . . . don't believe that. I can't."

"It would be really helpful if you would simply tell us where she's hidden them instead of floating around and creeping people out like some tormented Victorian spirit," Anya said sharply. "The only thing you're missing is a set of rattling chains."

"I cannot."

"You can't, or you *won't*?" Buffy demanded.

"It would make no difference," said the Ghost of Tara. *"Just as no one but Giles can release me from the Magic Box, you would not be able to gain entrance to the cave unless Willow deemed it so."*

Buffy's eyes narrowed. "So they're being held in a cave." Which was, really, not much help at all. There were dozens of the things around Sunnydale, and probably an equal amount that Buffy hadn't even discovered yet. "Which cave? Where?"

"I cannot see that," the Ghost of Tara said. Her eyes, transparent blue, looked oddly wise and innocent at the same time. *"They are in such . . . pain."*

A chill ran across Buffy's neck. "So they *are* hurt badly."

The Ghost of Tara started to reply, but her soft voice was drowned out by a groan at the table. Buffy and Anya turned and saw Oz pushing himself upright on the chair. When they turned back to the Ghost of Tara, she had disappeared again. "Well, that figures," Anya said in disgust as she scanned the room without success. "I was really hoping Tara hadn't fallen into the whole I'm-a-ghost-and-so-I-must-be-mysterious mentality."

At the table, Oz seemed to be finally coming back to his senses. "That sucked," he said hoarsely, then scrubbed at his face with the back of his hand. He looked anything but pleased at the dried blood that came off across his knuckles.

Buffy hurried over to him. "Are you all right?"

He nodded. "I remember . . . bits and pieces of what happened. I was just outside of town and was going to come by the Magic Box when I got zapped up to Willow's place, then whacked into perpetual werewolf mode." His face was white, his eyes shadowed and tired. There was something quietly disappointed about his expression. "She sure has changed."

Buffy looked from Oz to Anya, then back at Oz. She was *so* very furious at Willow, and yet . . . she still felt she had to explain her actions. Oz had once been loved by Willow, and he had loved—and maybe still did love—Willow back. Buffy couldn't bear for him to think that Willow had gone all dark-sided and evilly just for evil's sake. "It's because of what happened to Tara," Buffy told him softly.

Oz frowned. "What?"

"There were these three rotten techno-geeks," Anya said before Buffy could continued. "Their leader tried to shoot Buffy, and killed Tara instead."

Oz considered this, then nodded. "So now she's angry with Buffy."

"Well, no," Buffy said.

"Oh, I'm sure she is," Anya put in. "She skinned the leader—Warren—alive, then burned his body. Then she sucked all the power out of all the magick books in the shop and out of Giles, who came back from England to stop her, and now she's the most powerful Wiccan in the world." She paused and tilted her head. "She still can't find the other two, though. Too bad. If she could flay them, I think it might make her feel better."

"I don't understand," Oz said. He gestured to himself, his slender body beaten down from weeks of being held in permanent wolfness. "Why this?"

"I don't know," Buffy answered. "We thought she was trying to build power to do something terrible, then we found out—we *think*—that all she really wants is to bring Tara back from the dead."

"Can she do that?"

Anya shook her head. "From everything we can find out, no. Even Tara's ghost says it can't be done."

Oz's eyebrows raised. "Tara's *ghost*?"

"Oh, yeah," Buffy said. She sounded weary. "She's hanging around here too."

"The problem was that we didn't know that for sure, plus she was holding you and Spike—who has his soul back, by the way—prisoner," Anya said. "So Giles took the Ghost of Tara and forced it to stay in the Magic Box, and he told Willow that if she wanted to visit with it, she'd have to free you and Spike. And so here you are."

Oz rubbed his forehead as though he were trying to push away the last remnants of the tranquilizing drug. "Where's Giles?"

Buffy's expression darkened. "Well, we have this . . . problem."

"Willow's given Giles, Xander, and Dawn to a flesh-eating demon," Anya said in that amazing way she had of sounding bright even under the worst of circumstances. "Unless we give the Ghost of Tara back to her, it will continue to eat them alive. Except only Giles can release the Ghost of Tara, and so we're waiting to find out what Willow has to say about *that*."

Oz sat up straighter. "Continue to . . . ?" He left his question unfinished, then winced when he saw Buffy's small nod.

"You'll probably want to get clothed before Willow gets here," Anya said suddenly. "I know I'm quite uncomfortable around past lovers if I'm not properly dressed."

Poor Oz. He looked like it was all a bit too much for his brain to process. "Uh . . . sure."

"Giles always has an extra sweater and pair of slacks hanging in the back closet," Anya told him. "They'll be large on you, but at least then I can have my jacket back."

"Oh," Oz said, and glanced down. "Right." The Ghost of Tara was nowhere to be seen, but Oz still gave the room a final, thoughtful glance around before wobbling off to find Giles's spare set of duds.

Chapter Eleven

"They said *what?*"

At the tone of her voice, the sniveling little demon standing in front of Willow looked very much like he wanted to take a step—or maybe several hundred steps—back, but he didn't dare move. He cleared his throat, and she knew he was trying to find enough air to repeat himself. If he didn't get on with it, perhaps she'd help him by expanding his lungs to twelve times their normal size—just to be helpful, of course.

"They said Giles is the only one who can release the boundary spell, and that he has to be at the shop to do it or it won't work." He swallowed, then made himself continue. "So you, uh, have to . . . you know. Go to them and bring that Giles guy with you."

"I got that part, thanks," Willow snapped. Then her

eyes narrowed. "What else did you tell them? Perhaps the location of the cave?"

The demon shook his head hard enough to make the bones in his neck audibly pop. "No, no," he said. "It never even came up. I went in there saying right off the bat that if they tried to push me around, I wasn't saying anything. So they didn't." He actually looked rather proud of himself, enough so that Willow relaxed.

"All right," she said. She was seething inside, but she wasn't going to let the cowardly demon know just how much this latest snag had affected her. "Here." She tossed him a small velvet bag containing the agreed-upon amount of cash. "You're done."

The demon peeked inside the bag, then grinned. "If you have any other jobs—"

"I'll send for you," Willow interrupted. She made a *go away* gesture, and the demon wisely decided to take off.

After he was gone, she felt her fingers slowly tighten around the arms of the chair on which she'd been sitting, squeezing harder and harder until they were digging deep and splitting the surface of the plush velvet upholstery. The boundary spell—she'd remembered it, of course, but not the details. The *important* details: like the fact that even though she'd drained him of everything available at the time, Giles had replenished his power enough to cast an unbreakable spell, one that would keep Tara and her apart from now until the sky fell in if she didn't do what Buffy said. But she couldn't really blame Buffy for this one; oh no—this had been all Giles and his take-precautions-at-every-step-of-the-way attitude. She'd asked it before, but she couldn't help wondering again: *Why hadn't they just left her alone?*

Willow felt cool, bare wood pressing beneath her fingertips, and she pulled her fingers free of the puncture wounds she'd made in both the arms of her chair. Then she stood and squared her shoulders. It was time for the final step. She hadn't wanted to do it, but now she must. It didn't matter. It would only prove to them, and to herself, that she was strong enough to come face-to-face with the path she had chosen, as well as to confront its consequences. It was just another bump along the road to resurrecting Tara, but it wasn't a stop. Never that.

She was almost ready. Her coven would gather tonight for the final time, ready to turn over all the power they'd gathered to her, pour into her that final extra-heavy boost she would need. To show her gratefulness, they would be free to go; as far as she was concerned, they could use what they had learned in whatever manner they chose, be it good or evil or somewhere in the gray between. As long as she got her Tara back, it didn't matter to Willow what they did with the rest of their lives.

In the meantime, she had to pay another visit to the cave. And this one would have to end in bloodshed.

Like before, the smell of blood was thick in the air, palpable. This time, however, Willow was ready for it, would not let it affect her as it had on her first visit, when she'd seen the damage the Gnarl she'd created was doing to Xander and Dawn.

Or so she thought.

The two demons looked up in surprise as Willow passed her hand over the pentagram to let herself in, then re-created it—obviously they hadn't expected her to come back for a repeat visit. They seemed to be quite engaged in what they were doing, in their . . . buffets. The Gnarls backed up respectfully as she entered, still staying in the territory of their own meals, unknowingly making it easy for Willow to pinpoint which of the two almost-twins went with whom without having to insist they model for her. Staring down at their three victims—okay, let's be honest here: at *her* three victims—Willow found her stomach doing a nasty, involuntary roll, the warning signals of coming nausea.

Willow had been certain she would be ready for this. After all, she'd already seen what the first Gnarl had done to Dawn and Xander, so really, how much worse could it be?

Much, *much* worse.

If on her first visit the cave had smelled like blood, it now smelled like an abattoir, a place of slaughter and coming death. In only . . . what? An hour? Two? Just that little bit of time, and the second Gnarl had gone to work on Giles's belly with a vengeance, peeling and . . . *eating* at a rate Willow had never expected. Her mistake was obvious: The first Gnarl hadn't really gone at a slower pace at all. It just had two meals to choose from at one time, could divide its time, and

could gorge itself at a slower pace. Its brother, however, had no such double selection, and this creature
had chowed down on the helpless former Watcher at an
alarming rate.

Inside her coat, Willow found herself clenching
her fists—she seemed to be doing a lot of that lately—
so hard that her fingernails pushed painful crescents
into her palms. Xander and Dawn were quiet and
bloody, having likely succumbed to shock and the
chilly, circulation-slowing temperature of the cave
floor. Both stared at the ceiling as the original Gnarl
shot her a cautious glance, then inched over and began
delicately peeling another thin strip of skin from
Dawn, this one following the curve of one shoulder
and down her arm. As the creature worked it free and
held it up to admire it, Willow had to look away.

Giles . . . well, he was a mess. The Gnarl had
ripped open his jacket and shirt, and everything from
the blood-soaked waistband of his slacks to just where
the sides of his rib cage curved up toward the sternum
was an open, gaping wound—raw muscle glistening in
the glow of the torches that were set here and there
around the small cavern. The demon eating him was
much more impatient than its brother; it was working
its meal free in strips almost an inch wide and stuffing
them greedily into its leering mouth. When it saw the
first Gnarl resume its meal, it quickly resumed its own
dinner. At first it paid no attention to Willow as it bent
over and lapped noisily at the trail of blood leaking
from the latest wound in Giles's stomach. Then, as she
stepped closer, the thing lifted its face and growled at

her like a territorial dog, sending droplets of red spraying into the air in front of it. To really drive everything home, Giles moaned.

"You're done," she told the demon. "No more."

But the demon only laughed at her. "Silly witch, now he's mine, now until the end of dine."

Willow frowned, not sure if she'd heard the Gnarl correctly or if the word "dine" had been intentional. It didn't matter, because she had a different word to substitute. She took one hand out of her pocket and forced herself to flex the stiffened fingers. She tried to smile, but even she could feel that it came out more like a grimace. "I think you missed your rhyme," she said calmly. "I'm sure you meant to say 'end of *mine.*'" And she flung the two-inch shards of glass that had formed within her unseen grasp.

Her aim was perfect—of course—and the Gnarl never had a chance to duck. It screamed as the pieces plunged deeply into its eyes and pierced the brain, and its next move—the supremely stupid instinct of slapping its hands against its face—just helped matters nicely along. Death was nearly instantaneous.

On the ground, Giles blinked, then managed to move his head until he could see Willow. "Willow? I—"

The pain hit him.

The former Watcher was tough. To his credit, he didn't scream, and Willow couldn't say for sure that she would have been as quiet under the same circumstance. She hoped to God she'd never have to find out. Giles's mouth opened, but no sound came out; instead he brought his hand up fast and hard and jammed it into his mouth, muffling any sound that would have escaped. When the urge had passed, he slowly let his hand fall back to the cold dirt and he just lay there, chest heaving while everything inside him and below his rib cage was now exposed to the outside air.

"Need help," he managed. "Hospital . . . something." Giles turned his head just enough to where he could see Xander and Dawn lying so still a few feet away. Even that tiny movement made him gasp. "The others . . . too."

That curious pinging was back in her brain, that same ugly and disconcerting sort of déjà-vu sensation that she'd gotten the last time. To make it worse, every muscle in Willow's body was singing in sympathetic pain, but she could not, she *would* not, let him see that—she mustn't. It would show a weakness, and above all, until she got the Ghost of Tara back, she *must* be strong. "I'm afraid not," she said in as icy a voice as she could manage. "The best I can offer you is a ride back to the Magic Box."

"You are a two-faced gifty-giver," the first Gnarl said from directly behind her. She whirled just as it took a swipe toward her, but a snap of her fingers bent all of its claws backward nearly far enough to break them. The remaining demon screamed in agony and backed up. "You killed brother Gnarl!" it hissed. "Bad witch!"

"Go back to your meal before I do the same to you," Willow commanded. Shame washed over her. God, she couldn't believe she'd just told it to go on and keep eating away at Xander and Dawn, but there it was. She was gone, past the point of no return—a woman who could claim to possess a soul but who had no human heart or compassion left. How could she be anything but truly evil if she would do something like this to two people who had once been her friends? To *Xander*?

Something tugged gently at her ankle. When she looked down, Willow realized that Giles had draped one blood-covered hand across the top part of her foot. "Leave me for him," Giles said faintly. "Take them . . . instead."

She shook her head, then glared at the Gnarl until it backed away. "I can't do that, Giles. I need you back at the Magic Box to free the Ghost of Tara." She studied him for a second. "You did this," she finally told him. "You and Buffy. You forced my hand, and this is the result."

Giles blinked a couple of times, then he managed to focus on Willow's face. "No," he whispered. "You . . . made your own choices. We made you do nothing."

She waved his comment away, then reached down and grasped his wrist. The truth of his words rankled her, almost made her angry enough to yank him up. But . . . no. He just looked too awful, in more physical agony than perhaps she had ever imagined. She just couldn't bear to add to it. In the end, she just lifted his hand enough to hold on tight—

—and shimmered him away from the cave.

Oz had barely gotten the last of his borrowed outfit tightened enough to stay put when he heard the front door of the Magic Box slam open and a whole world of noise seemed to start out front.

He was bone tired, more exhausted than he had ever been in his life. Even studying the rigorous mental techniques necessary to maintain his humanness through a full moon hadn't taken this much out of him, and during those months there'd been times when he'd believed he was too tired to breathe. But now . . . God. Spending weeks and weeks as a werewolf had superset his metabolism and burned up energy and adrenaline that simply didn't exist in the natural genetic structure of his body. He felt as if he barely had the strength to thread one end of Giles's belt through the other and then work the buckle.

And, as was so common on the Hellmouth, yet another disaster was just a few steps away. He sucked in a deep breath, then headed toward the main room, using the wall to steady himself a couple of times. The length of the shop felt like miles, but Oz made it, and at the other end he came face-to-face with the woman he'd once loved—and perhaps still did love in some part of his heart—and who had damned near turned him into a forever-version of the thing he wanted most in the world *not* to be.

Willow.

She wasn't actually *inside* the Magic Box. He hadn't gotten all the details, but Oz had managed to glean that Giles had put a serious no-trespassing spell on the ins and outs of the building. Because of this, she was standing just outside the door, and there was something crumpled on the ground at her feet.

Oz couldn't remember everything that had happened to him since she'd kidnapped him, but staring at her now brought back bits and pieces, flashes of everything from confusion to pain to hunger to a sense of rage that never seemed to stop and was infused inside every bone in his body. His only memory of his first night in her loft was short and filled with bewildered questions—life had been going along just fine, then *wham*! There he was, dazed and at the end of some magick-soaked chain. As freakazoid as that recollection was, it was infinitely preferable to the fragmented memories that followed. At the time, he hadn't understood what was going on, but now, of course, he did: The dark forces of nature had never intended that he—or anyone—be a perpetual werewolf, and sometimes, on the rarest of occasions, Oz would almost regain himself again. Against Willow's incredible power, of course, and being so close within her sphere of influence, he'd never been able to truly break free.

In retrospect, that was probably just as well, because he would have only been stranded at the end of an impossible-to-break magickal chain. It had taken being away from her, *far* enough away, for his own true human nature to reassert itself. For all the time he'd been imprisoned, Oz had only pieces of memories that had anything to do with actually seeing Willow. They were like strange, razor-edge shards of mirrored glass that had whirled in his mind, showing first one side, then the other: blackness, a glimpse of Willow's face, blackness, a glimpse, on and never-endingly on. Even toward the end, when his human mind had processed what had happened to him and finally had begun to overpower the screams of the beast within him, Oz had never truly accepted the Willow he was seeing now, banned from the Magic Box and screaming just a few feet away from him.

Willow's face was twisted with rage, and her black-lipped mouth was drawn back in a terrible grimace. Her hair and eyes were as black as her mouth, and veins wove their way across the skin of her face and hands like a demon-child's horrific Magic Marker drawings. The soft and beautiful Willow he'd once known had been replaced, *consumed,* by a powerful, fury-soaked Wiccan who no longer knew—or cared— that he was alive.

"Here's what you get! You took Tara TWICE, Buffy—once by your stupidity in not taking care of Warren, and then after her death. You couldn't even leave her ghost *alone!"*

Buffy was there, standing next to a cringing Anya and apparently incapable of doing anything except listen. For some reason, both women seemed nearly paralyzed; their heads were the only things that moved as they stared from the bundle on the ground to Willow, then back again. Around them, the speed of the howling wind increased and the temperature dropped.

"Well, here's what you demanded!" Incredibly, Willow's voice rose even louder, like an ill-contained mini-tornado. Even though she couldn't come in, the effect was still felt; here and there around the shop, a few of the glass panes along the cabinet doors showed sudden cracks zinging across their surface.

"Do you still think I'm KIDDING when I tell you to give her back?" Willow screeched. *"If you do, ask Giles about what's happening to Xander and Dawn. Ask him what it's like to be eaten ALIVE!"* Her gaze flicked to the thing she'd brought with her, then back to Buffy and Anya. *"You have two hours, and no more. One to clean* him *up, and one more to GIVE TARA BACK TO ME!"*

Her words ended on a howl, and Willow slammed her wrists together in an X formation, then yanked them apart. The motion sent her image blasting upward—rather than disappearing or teleporting away, her body shot into the air like a smear of black, like the shadow of speed itself as it moved. Then she was finally gone, and there was silence.

Well, not quite.

The blood-drenched thing curled on the concrete moaned.

Buffy bolted forward, with Anya right on her heels. It took Oz's exhausted mind a good ten seconds to process what he was seeing, and even then he couldn't quite believe it, couldn't really accept that Willow would do this to someone, not *this,* not to *Giles,* albeit who in different ways than he and Buffy and Tara, had been so much a part of her life.

"Giles? Can you hear me?" Crouched in the doorway, Buffy reached out to touch his shoulder, then recoiled as she realized that the sea of red along his stomach was actually a sheet of raw muscle. "Oh, my *God.*"

"Wow," Anya said. Her eyes were wide with surprise. "He's really hurt."

"Get him inside," Oz said from behind him. "We've got to get him covered up and take him to a hospital, maybe call an ambulance. He's probably in shock."

It took them a few minutes of struggling, with Oz doing less pulling and more hovering than Buffy and Anya—he just didn't have enough of his strength back yet. Ultimately, they had the former Watcher stretched out on a blanket on the floor, and the three of them knelt by his side. No one knew what to say, or maybe they just couldn't speak. Giles was terribly injured, and if Oz had thought he'd had it bad by being imprisoned for a few weeks, he now felt like he ought to count himself as having been damned lucky in the Willow Lottery.

"We can't fix this," Anya finally said. Seeing Giles in this bad a shape seemed to have blasted all the sarcasm out of her. "This is much worse than I would ever expect a mortal to be able to survive." She looked from Giles's mutilated torso to Buffy, then swallowed. "I . . ." For a moment, she almost couldn't continue. "Xander? And Dawn? Do you think they're like this too?"

"Must . . . get them . . . out."

All three of them jerked when they realized Giles was actually talking. Buffy leaned over him. "Giles, did you see them? Were they . . . with you, wherever you were? With the same, uh, thing going on."

"Yes . . ." Buffy fought the urge to scream in frustration as his eyes drifted closed. Then suddenly he forced them open again.

Relief rippled across Buffy's nerves, and she grimaced. "Where are they? Anya and Oz'll take you to the hospital, and I'll go and get them."

"Can't get in," Giles said faintly. "Spell on the door, demon inside. Demon . . . eating. Their kind . . ." He paused long enough to make all three of them nervous. "They paralyze their . . . food."

Something inside Buffy ran cold, and she couldn't remember the last time she'd felt so helpless, so unable to go to the aid of the people she loved most.

"Must give her . . . Tara," Giles whispered. "Must release . . . the boundary spell."

Buffy shook her head. "If we don't get you medical attention—"

Giles pulled in air, then wheezed in pain. "Doctor . . . later. Get me up."

"Bad idea," Oz said.

"Spell is easy to . . . let go," Giles managed. "Just need . . . Tara, her ghost."

"I'm here."

Buffy scowled as the Ghost of Tara seemed once again to pop up out of nowhere.

The spirit looked devastated as she stared down at Giles. *"I am so very sorry for you. I'm afraid Willow's goals have clouded her judgment."*

"Well, she's not the only one that's ever happened to," Buffy said. Her voice hardened. "But this time, it's gotten my sister in trouble."

"And Xander," Anya put in.

"Right." Buffy slipped a hand under Giles's shoulder. "Are you sure about this, Giles? You're bleeding. A *lot*."

"Yes," he gasped. "Must sit . . . up and say the incantation."

Anya looked at him dubiously, but there wasn't much she could say. "How far up?" she finally asked. "Up on the floor, or all the way up on a chair? 'Cause if it's the chair, that's going to be hard for you."

"Floor . . . will do."

"Shortest distance between up and down," Oz said. He was feeling a bit better, although he was a long way from recovered. At least he now thought he could contribute to the Giles project: get one of the chairs over to Giles so that he'd have something to lean against when they pulled him up. Oz didn't want to think about how much more horribly the man's stomach was going to hurt when they started moving him upright and all those bare muscles started contracting.

Buffy eyed Giles and the chair. "I don't think he's going to stay," she said. "He's weak from loss of blood."

Anya got up and went behind the counter. In a few seconds, she was back with a length of cotton rope in her hands. "Here," she said. "We can put this under his arms and use it to hold him against the chair." She looked at Giles. "Are you ready?"

"Yes," Giles said, although he sounded anything but. His voice was bubbly, like there was fluid in his lungs, and his skin was chalk-white. His eyes rolled in his head until his pain-clouded gaze focused on the Ghost of Tara. "You tell her," he rasped, "Xander and Dawn go . . . free. That's part of the . . . deal."

Buffy swallowed and touched his arm, trying to be

gentle. "Giles, are they hurt like . . . like you? Are they hurt that badly? Where can I find them?"

"I couldn't tell," he admitted. His voice seemed smoother, but they could all tell it was costing him an immense amount of effort to keep it that way. "But . . . yes. I think they must be. They're at St. Dominic Savio Cemetery, somewhere around the far eastern corner. My car might still be there. . . ."

Buffy squeezed her eyes shut briefly, then opened them. "Then let's get on with it. Let's get this spell thingy over and done with so we can take care of the rest of this . . . problem."

Oz ran his tongue over his teeth. Despite washing his mouth out in the bathroom, he thought he could still taste blood. "All right."

After a little fumbling around to find the right position, the three of them were in the best places they could guess at to get Giles into the seated position he wanted so badly. "Get ready," Anya said matter-of-factly. "He's probably going to get loud."

"Let's just do it," Buffy said. "One, two, *three*."

As quickly and smoothly as they could, they lifted the top half of Giles's body into a seated position.

And he screamed like a man being tortured.

There was nothing girlish or high about the noise—it was full-throated and masculine, and it seemed, at least in the ears of the people who cared about him, to go on forever. When it finally ended, they thought he'd passed out—a man in enough agony to scream like that, how could he have done otherwise?

But no, he'd just run out of lung power, and as he

sat there with his back against the chair and the rope holding him up, his skin actually went corpse-gray.

"He's not dead, is he?" Anya asked anxiously. "Gray is a terrible color on him."

"No," Oz said. "I think he *is* unconscious, though." He looked from Giles to Buffy.

She stood there, her mind spinning with indecision. Giles's injuries were so far beyond anything they could help him with that they *had* to get him some help, but if they took him out of this building, he wouldn't be able to release the Ghost of Tara. If Willow's demand wasn't met, their chances of finding Xander and Dawn were hosed. Giles had said she wouldn't be able to get into the tomb where they were stuck—even if she could find it to begin with—because of Willow's spell on the entrance. Having run into that repeatedly at her former friend's current living quarters, Buffy was through being stubborn enough to think she could circumvent Willow's magicks.

So she could sit here and possibly watch the unconscious Giles bleed to death and die, which would mean Xander and Dawn would probably die.

Or she could take him to the hospital. Which meant Xander and Dawn would probably die . . . but at least Giles might live.

Buffy thought her heart was going to shatter, but she had to make the only choice she could under the circumstances:

"Call an ambulance and grab your coats."

Chapter Twelve

Giles came back to consciousness just as Anya was finishing on the telephone.

"You have to come quickly. He was attacked by . . . something. No, I don't know what. But he's bleeding. A lot."

From the corner of his eye, Giles saw Buffy standing next to him, and managed to find enough strength to reach for her wrist. She jumped at his touch.

"Giles? Hang on—the ambulance is on its way." She knelt next to him, and he realized Oz was on his other side. "We're going to have to untie you so the paramedics don't see the ropes."

"Not—" He coughed, and the pain was excruciating, like having a sheet of burning napalm spread across the muscles of his stomach. It took all his willpower not to scream. He had to remain focused.

Too much was at stake. It would take every sliver of energy he had to do the release spell, quickly, before the paramedics arrived. "Yet," he finished. He squeezed his eyes shut and concentrated on forming his words, not choking or mumbling or stuttering with pain. "Bring me the . . . jar. Tara's jar."

Buffy stared at him, and dimly he realized she had tear streaks down her face. "Giles, you can't—you need to reserve your strength."

"Here," Anya said, and pushed it into his hands. At Buffy's glare, she shrugged. "He could die anyway. You might as well let him try to do something worthwhile as his last act."

"Always the Queen of Tact," Oz commented dryly.

Giles ignored them and closed his hand around the jar, brought his other hand up, and lifted the lid. "Tara—"

"I'm still here, Giles. I haven't left you."

"I need sand," he told Anya, "in a bowl. And draw the same runes for me. Do you remember them?" He'd managed to say three full sentences, and he felt like he'd run ten miles.

"Yes," she said, but her voice sounded very far away, and things were starting to go gray around the edges.

"Here." Anya's voice cut through his thoughts, although he didn't know if the sound of it was bringing him back from the edge of unconsciousness or from an actual blackout. "The sand. I've drawn the runes in it, just like you said."

Giles's eyelids fluttered open, and he found himself looking directly at the bowl of sand. It was long and shallow, and he could see the runes etched in it that represented a woman—Tara—and a man—himself—plus the one that represented a journey. "Now we need the circle." His voice grated. "And a line between the two."

Anya frowned, then her expression brightened. "Oh—sure. Like this." She made an admirably smooth circle around the figures, then joined them with a horizontal line. "There," she said with satisfaction.

Oz, still at Giles's side, suddenly looked up. "I can hear the ambulance's siren," he said. "It's only two or three blocks away. You'd better hurry." Although the rest of them couldn't hear a thing, they had no doubt that Oz, with his sensitive werewolf hearing, was right.

Giles swallowed. Then it would have to be short and simple, and he hoped the spell would work. He inhaled, and thought he could feel pain all the way down to his soul. It didn't help knowing that if he failed, Xander and Dawn would continue to endure the same pain, right up until they, mercifully, died. "Tara," he said, "I release you from the boundaries of the Magic Box and return you to this crystal holding jar." He reached out a shaking hand and rubbed away the line connecting the male and female runes, then completely obliterated the mark representing travel. "From this jar . . ." A breeze stirred the room as the Ghost of Tara's specter began to shift. Giles blinked and fought to concentrate as the draft brought fresh pain across his exposed stomach. Somehow he made himself keep going. "From this jar you will be traded for Xander and

Dawn, or within the very essence of its molecules you will stay forever."

The Ghost of Tara's face showed her surprise, then suddenly her form swirled to a thin line and was sucked into the crystal teardrop jar. Giles put the top on it as best he could and pushed it toward Buffy, who finished sealing the jar. A bright red glow rotated through the front window of the Magic Box as the ambulance pulled up outside.

"Get the ropes off him," Buffy ordered right before the paramedics began pounding on the locked front door. "Toss them behind the counter." She tightened the lid on the jar, then slid it into the side pocket of her jacket.

Anya knelt and began prying at the loose knots. "Giles, what if something goes wrong? What if either one . . ." She didn't finish.

"No time for—arrrgh!" The ropes undone, he slid downward in the seat, painfully ending his thought. Anya threw the ropes out of sight. Just in time, too— Oz had gone over to answer the door and had barely turned the lock before the medics burst through and rushed over to Giles. Then the questions started:

"What happened to him?"

"Is he related? Your father?"

"He's going to need a transfusion. Do you know his blood type?"

"Do you have emergency information for him? Is there someone to contact?"

"Is he on any medication?"

"Does he have any health problems?"

Dozens more, too many at once, and later, neither Buffy, Anya, nor Oz would remember how they answered them all. While one paramedic covered the wet and raw expanse of Giles's stomach with a half-dozen oversize nonstick pads, then draped them with a single layer of a sheet to keep the pads from blowing away, the other went back to the ambulance for a collapsible cart. The worst part of the entire ordeal was watching them lift Giles's limp figure from the floor to the cart—a mere six inches at most, but the pain from the motion was enough to send him back into unconsciousness. And maybe, considering how much red was already seeping through the pads and sheet, that was a blessing in not so much disguise.

"You can't all go with him," one of the paramedics told them when the three of them had anxiously clustered around the back of the ambulance. "There's room for only one person."

"I'll go," Oz said. "Buffy needs to go get Xander and Dawn. Anya—"

"I can get there on my own," Anya said quickly. She suddenly realized that Oz had no idea she'd gone back to being a vengeance demon. He'd missed the whole left-at-the-altar fiasco, and now was certainly not the time for a recap of the latest episodes of *The Xander and Anya Show*. "I'll be there soon."

He nodded and, in usual minimalist fashion—some things never change—climbed into the waiting ambulance without saying good-bye. The paramedics quickly closed the ambulance doors and, with lights and sirens blaring, sped away for Sunnydale Hospital.

Buffy didn't need any more time to get moving. "Come on, Anya," she said. "Let's go."

Anya stared at her. "What? You don't really expect me to go anywhere near Willow now, do you?"

"Yes. I can't drag them both back by myself, now can I?"

"Oh." Anya opened her mouth to protest, then pressed her lips together. "Right. I'll get my keys."

"I don't think I'll ever learn to like cemeteries in the middle of the night," Buffy said, staring around her. She was sure she'd been here before—she'd patrolled every cemetery in Sunnydale—but it was so small and old and abandoned that it had probably been years since she'd bothered. They'd found Giles's car fairly easily. Leaves had settled into the bed of its hood where the windshield met the body, as though the car had been parked there for months rather than a few hours. The cemetery was completely dark—no streetlights—and there was only a sliver of moon overhead. Anya had retrieved a couple of flashlights out of the trunk of her car, but they didn't do much; instead they reminded her of the way a person uses a laser pointer to tease a cat.

"Where do we start?" she asked Buffy. "This place looks deserted. They could hide anywhere."

Buffy looked around the shadowed grounds thoughtfully. Inside her coat, she couldn't help running her fingers over the crystal jar that contained what remained of Tara, that elusive spiritual essence that Willow wanted so badly, she would be willing to torture her former friends to get it back. "Maybe not. Figure you're dragging people in and out, you'll want to be close to the road—especially if someone else is doing your dirty work for you. I'm thinking the tomb we want is pretty close."

Anya said nothing, just continued to poke unhappily among the headstones. Did anyone take notice of this old cemetery anymore? It didn't look like the graves had been visited in decades, and clearly there was no groundskeeper—the place was full of weeds and rocks, the bushes were overgrown, and it had been so long since the trees had been cut back that some of the limbs were literally dragging against the ground. The place was like something out of a black-and-white movie of "The Legend of Sleepy Hollow." All it needed was a—

"Vampire!" Buffy yelled.

"What?" Anya turned back. Something small and skinny hit her from the side. She stumbled and lost her balance, falling over a crumbled headstone. The tackling bloodsucker came right down with her.

Incredibly, the vampire snapped at her, trying to get to her throat. "Oh, get off of me, you idiot!" Anya swatted the thing aside hard enough to make it whine. "Can't you tell I'm a demon?"

Instead of listening, the scrawny little bloodbeast came at her a third time. Angry now, Anya morphed into vengeance demon and snarled at it; that was enough to make it pause. The creature was emaciated and filthy—had that nasty creature actually *touched* her?—and she couldn't even tell if it was male or female. Obviously starving, its common sense had apparently been eaten away ages ago along with its body fat.

It glared at her uncertainly. "Blood," it whined. "I can smell it . . . somewhere." It sniffed the air frantically, like a hunting dog trying to catch a scent. "Hungry," it continued, then suddenly jerked its head toward Buffy. "You—human! *Food!*"

But Buffy only looked annoyed. She just didn't have time for this right now. "No. Me Slayer," she said as the vampire rushed her. "You dead." One neat jab, and the thing was out of its misery—and hers—for good. She kept her stake and slipped it back into her other pocket.

"Well," Anya said. "That was very anticlimactic."

"If only more things were." Buffy squinted at the darkness. "Our once-upon-a-vamp said he'd smelled blood," she said. "I'm going to take that as a positive sign that we're close."

Anya inhaled deeply. "Yeah, I can smell it now." She stepped around Buffy, then chose a direction. "This way. Look." She pointed at the ground, and they could both see a path, very faint but still evident, that had been beaten along the dry grass, dead leaves, and dirt.

Anya let Buffy step around her and take the lead, and even in the blackness, Buffy didn't miss her distressed look. "What?"

"It's getting stronger," Anya admitted. "A *lot* stronger. I know that means we're close to finding them, but—"

"What?" Buffy demanded again.

"I've just never . . . smelled so much of it coming from anyone who was actually, you know. Still alive."

Buffy swallowed, wishing Anya hadn't said that. She'd been trying to mentally prepare herself for the possibility of the worst, of course, but she wasn't having much success. The idea that Willow would actually kill Xander and Dawn was . . . unthinkable. And if Willow *had* killed them and therefore couldn't make the trade that Giles had worked into his incantation, she'd be punished by never getting the Ghost of Tara. It was no comfort at all. No, Buffy had to cling to the hope that she wasn't too late. She—

"It's right over there," Anya said suddenly, pointing toward an even darker spot in the darkness.

—didn't think she'd be able to bear it if she walked into that tomb and found two lifeless bodies. The thought nearly made Buffy nauseated, and for a moment she wasn't sure if she'd have to throw up before she could go inside. But, no—she was tough; she *had* to be. Out here was nothing; the real test was still ahead.

The tomb itself was pretty standard stuff: old and crumbling, worn enough so that the dates had been smoothed away by the wind, rain, and the passage of time. It didn't appear to be that big, but Buffy wasn't deceived; these things usually had some kind of ratty staircase leading down into God knows what. It was a good bet that this one wasn't going to be any kind of exception.

The outside door came open easily enough—suspiciously easily, in fact. That meant Willow wasn't worried about her or anyone else getting inside . . . but what about what was inside getting *out*? A valid question, but she needn't have dwelled on it. Shining their flashlights around the inside of the tiny building revealed only one burial alcove— quite a lonely existence for whoever had been interred here, with "had been" being the operative words. The alcove contained a concrete container that had long ago been broken open. The requisite staircase was right in the middle of the room, a hole in the floor surrounded by a tarnished copper railing, leading downward into blackness.

And now even Buffy could smell the blood.

Its scent was thick and sickly, *decaying*—so different from what she was used to smelling in her hundreds of blood 'n' guts battles. Buffy inhaled automatically, then gagged before she could stop herself. It took a precious ten seconds to force her body to get a grip, then she was able to block off her nose and breathe through her mouth. "Let's go," she said grimly. Her voice, slightly nasal, echoed unpleasantly in the tiny mausoleum.

Anya nodded stiffly, but Buffy thought it was more nervousness over Willow and what they might find than the blood smell. Anya had chalked up more than a thousand years of messy destruction, and Buffy was sure the vengeance demon had quite the tolerance for the scented side of her dirty deeds. That said, Anya followed Buffy down the stairs, straining to see in the darkness. It didn't take much—five or six steps and they could make out the glow of firelight farther down, getting brighter with each stair. The bottom of the staircase faced a doorway; beyond it the torchlight glowed brightest, but when Buffy tried to step through, she hit . . . nothing. Blocking her way was an invisible brick wall, a force field, whatever you wanted to call it. She couldn't go any farther.

"Willow has a spell on it," Anya told her, tentatively touching the invisible barrier, "much like the one that Giles put on the Magic Box. You won't be able to get in until she disables it." She was silent for a moment. "She probably made it so, uh, whatever's inside can't get out either."

"So generous of her," Buffy muttered. She could have pounded the wall in frustration. "Then where *is* she?"

And with utterly perfect timing, Willow stepped into view on the other side of the doorway.

Chapter Thirteen

Buffy and Willow stared at each other, and for a long moment, neither moved. Finally, Willow broke the silence. "Tara," she said flatly. "Where is she?"

Buffy pulled the crystal teardrop jar out of her pocket and held it up. "Right here."

Willow jabbed a finger toward the ground. "Leave her there and go."

But Buffy shook her head and slipped the small jar back into her jacket. "No can do," she said. "You have to release Xander and Dawn."

"I will."

Buffy stood her ground. "Giles's release spell ties Tara's freedom to their release. You can't have one without the other."

Willow's mouth turned down. "You and Giles," she said. "You just keep pushing, don't you?"

"Hey," Anya said, "I think you took your pound of flesh from him."

Willow's head swiveled in Anya's direction, and her eyes were dangerously black—ominous enough to make Anya take a step backward.

Buffy spread her hands. "It's not such a hard thing, Willow. And Anya's right: You hurt Giles terribly." Her eyes narrowed. "Is it the same with Xander and Dawn? Were you that vicious?"

Willow laughed hollowly. "You call me vicious when everything you've done has destroyed parts of *my* life. Better take a look at your own glass house before you start pitching stones, Buffy."

Buffy exhaled. "I'm not here to argue with you. If you want Tara, you have to let me take Xander and Dawn out of here."

Willow glanced over her shoulder, then back at Buffy and Anya. "I'm afraid that decision isn't totally up to me. But you can certainly give it your best try." She waved her hand at one side of the doorway, and the pentagram blasted into the stone at the bottom glowed for a moment, then disappeared. "Come on in."

Buffy didn't need a second invitation. She went through the door at full speed, got two feet in, then came to a sudden stop, staring at the ground in horror.

Her sister was there, as was Xander. They'd been placed on the floor, end to end, with their feet almost touching. Something inside her had hoped against all odds that Willow hadn't really done this, that what had happened to Giles had been nothing more than a horrible mistake wrongly blamed on Willow, and nothing of the sort would have actually been done to Xander, and certainly not to her beautiful baby sister. But now . . .

God.

"Don't take too long to dwell on the bad," Willow said. Her voice was like a frozen river. "I'm perfectly willing to abide by Giles's spell and trade them for the return of the Ghost of Tara, but I'm afraid they don't really belong to me anymore."

"What?" Dazed, Buffy forced herself to look away from the wet, red mass that made up most of Xander's stomach—like Giles's—and the raw wound that cut across most of Dawn's upper body. Their eyes were glazed with shock, staring toward the ceiling, and even as outrage settled over Buffy, the very back of her mind whispered that neither had very long to live. "They're not yours. . . . What are you talking about?"

"I gave them away." Willow inclined her head jerkily toward a shadow against the far wall. "Xander and Dawn belong to the Gnarl now. Only its death will release them from their paralysis." She stared at Buffy. "Of course, when the paralysis is gone—*if* you can kill the Gnarl—they'll start feeling the pain. Not much to be done about that."

Buffy automatically followed the direction of Willow's gaze, but she couldn't see much of anything besides the shadows dancing in the firelight. . . . No, wait—there *was* something moving in there, a darker shape among the shadows. Was that a face, slipping quickly across the wall?

"Of course," Willow continued, "if the creature catches you with one of its fingernails, you'll be paralyzed just like Xander and Dawn. And you'll be its third meal."

Anya, who had wisely stayed outside the cave door, poked her head inside, looking around nervously to make sure the Gnarl wasn't within range. "The terms of Giles's spell specifically require a trade," she reminded Willow. "If that happens, you'll never get Tara back."

Incredibly, Willow only shrugged. "I think that eventually I'll find a way," she said. "Tara's spirit will always be out there somewhere."

Buffy shook her head in bewilderment. "But you don't know that for sure. You'd take that chance? *Why?*"

Suddenly Willow's eyes blazed. "For *payback,* that's why! You think that you can waltz in here, after taking the last of anything at all that was meaningful in my life, and not have to at least *work* a little to get what you want?" She gave a strident laugh. "Not this time. Now you get to re-evaluate the consequences of your great and wonderful Slayerness, the fallout from you always thinking you're right and the rest of the world is wrong and be damned to anyone who stands in your righteous little way!" Her expression was so furious that the blue-black veins visible under her skin had darkened to a thick, almost markerlike intensity. "It's time to realize that other people get *hurt* as you go blasting through life, Buffy! Time to reap what you've sown so that *you* know how the rest of us feel!"

"But *this,*" Buffy whispered. "To hurt your friends—"

"Would you *please* take yourself off repeat?" Willow asked bitingly. "I've heard this at least a dozen times, and I'm sick of it. It doesn't change anything." She glanced around the cavern, then waved her hand at the doorway again. The bottom pentagram reappeared, sealing Buffy inside and Anya out. "I'm through listening to you," Willow said flatly. "The pentagram disappears when the demon is dead. The Gnarl is willing to fight for its supper. Are you willing to fight to take its supper from it?"

And—

snap

—Willow was gone.

An instant later, Buffy instinctively dropped into a crouch as from behind her something long and sharp whizzed across the space where her head had been.

She fell forward and onto her forearms, kicked her legs out behind her, then yanked her feet together and spun on the ground. With its legs caught between her ankles, the demon tumbled sideways and crashed hard to the dirt, squalling in surprise. It squirmed forward and tried to flail at her, intent on getting her with one of its poison-tipped fingernails; with her legs still pinning the creature's, Buffy rolled again, hard. The Gnarl's knees bent and went sideways at an angle they were never meant to go, and its growling turned into an agonized scream as both kneecaps dislocated. The beast tried to roll away from her and ended up pinned facedown on the ground, with Buffy on its back. As it fought to get its arms underneath in an effort to throw her off, Buffy yanked a stake out from the inside of her jacket—always helpful to have a Mr. Pointy around, no matter what the evening's plans—and rammed it as hard as she could into the back of the Gnarl's neck, just below the base of the thing's skull.

The demon convulsed beneath her, fingers digging into the rock-strewn dirt. For a moment, it looked like it was actually going to be able to get up—Buffy felt her body start to lift upward, like she was riding some kind of circus animal. Not good, so she balled up her fist and used it like a hammer, beating on the stake over and over again until it came out the front of the creature's throat and lodged into the ground. The Gnarl stiffened for an overlong moment, then finally went limp.

"Bravo!" Anya said, clapping from the doorway. "Great job—it's nearly impossible to avoid those disgustingly toxic fingernails!" As she said the last word, the locking pentagram at the bottom of the doorway suddenly glowed and disappeared; Anya glanced at it, then extended a finger cautiously in front of her. "Great," she said, then hurried into the cavern. "You'll need help carrying them." She halted, then looked down at Dawn and Xander and swallowed. "Oh . . ."

Buffy smacked the stake in the back of the Gnarl's neck a final time, just to be sure, then clambered off it and went to where her sister was stretched out on the ground. They were silent, unmoving. "The Gnarl's dead. Why aren't they moving, Anya? *Why aren't they moving?*"

"I . . . I don't know," Anya said in a choked voice. She knelt next to Xander and pushed the hair off his forehead. His eyes weren't closed, but they weren't open, and she found the effect terrifyingly like that of a corpse laid out on a metal table.

"Dawn?" Buffy raised her voice, trying to get it loud but not screaming, not yet . . . although there was a very good chance that that's where she was headed. "Dawn, can you hear me?" Her eyes were wide as she found Anya's gaze. "Do you think they could still be paralyzed?" A strange thing to hope for, but the best she could manage under the circumstances.

Anya blinked, then looked over to where the Gnarl was pinned facedown on the ground. It didn't move, didn't breathe; brackish body fluids had already spilled onto the ground from its mouth and the hole punched through its neck. "No—the Gnarl is dead. Its hold on them is broken." She looked back at Xander, then bent over until she could put her ear close to his mouth. After a few seconds, she relaxed a little. "He's not dead," she finally said. "I think they're in shock, or maybe a coma." She rubbed the back of her hand across her mouth, then looked at Buffy. "This is quite serious. They're so badly injured—I don't know how we're going to move them."

"I'll help," said an unsteady voice from the doorway.

"Spike!" Buffy said. "You're . . . walking."

"Talking, even." The blond vampire was as drawn and pale as she'd ever seen him, but at least he was upright and another hand to pitch in. "Checked out the old Watcher's car out there," he said, then held up his hand. A set of keys dangled from his fingers. "'E's lucky it wasn't stolen. Found these in the ignition."

"We'll get them into the car," Buffy decided, "and take them to the hospital. We can put Xander in Anya's car, and Dawn in Giles's. It's our only choice."

Spike came over to crouch next to Xander. "Looks like the man's paid for anything and everything he's ever done wrong with tonight's gig," he commented, then looked over at Dawn. "And then some. Shame about your sister. I'm thinking that's gonna leave a right nasty set of scars."

"I can't worry about that right now," Buffy said grimly. "First on the list is keeping them alive."

"Hop to it, then." Spike leaned over to slide his arms beneath Xander's shoulders and knees. "I've got bloody boy here. You and Anya handle baby sister as gently as you can."

Buffy nodded, but it wasn't as simple as it sounded. The skin across the expanse of Dawn's collarbone and upper chest was just . . . *gone,* and while at first she'd planned to slip her hands under her sister's shoulders while Anya took Dawn's feet, a second look told her that if she did that, she'd be gripping raw, skinless muscle. God, that *had* to hurt.

Spike hesitated, then paused long enough to pull off his long leather coat. He tossed it to Buffy. "Use this as a sling," he said. "One of you on each side, and we ought to be able to get them to the car." Buffy nodded and carefully lifted Dawn's upper body so Anya could spread the coat beneath her. Without waiting to be told, Spike bent and gathered Xander into his arms, then stood at the same time Buffy and Anya finally got his coat into position and lifted Dawn off the floor.

They even managed five steps toward the door before Xander and Dawn came to and started screaming in agony.

Buffy wasn't sure how many hours had passed before she realized that in her pocket she still had the crystal teardrop jar containing the Ghost of Tara.

She was sitting in the patients' waiting room with Oz, Anya, and Spike, feeling grubby and exhausted, mentally devastated, when she shifted on her chair and felt the lump in her jacket pocket. The trip up the tomb's stairs and to the car had been full of screaming and fighting, with both Dawn and Xander turning into writhing bundles as they tried uselessly to escape their own bodies. It didn't matter how she and the others had tried to quiet the two victims, and, of course, no amount of soothing did any good. The car had smelled of blood and panic and something darker that Buffy tried desperately not to think about: possible death. The ordeal had passed into the realm of unbelievable at the hospital, when both Xander and Dawn had continued to scream nonstop— how could two people so injured find the strength to keep going like that? Buffy didn't know, but then she also acknowledged that she didn't know anything, not really, about the level of torment they were enduring. Finding out from Oz that Giles had gone through the same thing—worse, actually, since "his" Gnarl had had only him upon which to satisfy its appetite—just added to the shock value of it all. It had taken heavy doses of morphine to drop them into pain-free unconsciousness so they could be examined by the horrified doctors.

And then another round of questions had started.

No one had thought to fabricate a story ahead of time, some tale that would support one another's and, somehow, explain these awful injuries. As it turned out, they hadn't done so badly on their own. Oz had simply said that he'd just arrived back in town and stopped by the Magic Box to say hello . . . where he'd found Giles on the floor and Anya and Buffy trying to help him. Beyond that he was ignorant of what had happened, and he was sticking safely to that statement. Anya, Buffy, and Spike maintained that they'd been on their way to the hospital—the paramedics hadn't paid any attention to them when they'd left the Magic Box—and had found Xander and Dawn on the way, crumpled on the side of the street; the dirt and grime encrusted in their clothes from lying on the tomb's floor at least somewhat supported that.

Still, the cops—called immediately by the hospital staff—were suspicious and jumpy. Buffy didn't think the local law enforcement actually thought *they* had done anything, but there were hushed discussions about serial this, and pattern that, all the strange goings-on that had increased in town over the past month or so. If only they knew the truth.

Now it was just Buffy and the others, waiting for the next bit of news about how the three patients were doing. All three had been listed in critical condition, and if there was such a thing as stages of critical, Buffy knew that Giles would be the worst among them. The doctors had been unsympathetically frank about their chances—blood loss was extensive; the wounds were open and right now there was no way to close them up; it would take months of skin grafts to repair the damage on all three. And with all that was the one brutal caveat: *if* they pulled through.

The trip from the tomb to the hospital had taken its toll on the rescuers, too, so no one had said anything for quite some time. Oz and Spike hadn't been around back then, but Buffy remembered the last time she and Anya had been here, when Giles had been brought in after his huge fight with Willow. She'd gotten the best of him—face it, she'd been getting the best of everyone since going the Wiccan equivalent of nuclear—and nearly paralyzed him for life; Anya's spell, which had taken two tries to get right, had restored feeling to his legs and normalcy to his life. Anya hadn't said anything in that arena yet, but somehow Buffy doubted that the injuries this time around were within the Anya-fixable range.

"I'll be right back," Buffy told the others, and inclined her head toward the ladies' room. As Buffy got up, they all went back to studying the floor or the wall or whatever other thing was currently the object of their stare.

Compared to the waiting room it serviced, the restroom wasn't big, but it was—at least for now—conveniently empty. Buffy pulled the crystal jar from her pocket and set it on the counter between the two sinks, then stared at it. The counter was dark-colored laminate, and the jar glittered starkly on its surface, reflecting back at Buffy in the mirror. She was more than a little shocked at her own image. The young woman in the mirror looked older and exhausted, beaten into the ground by life and a whole host of problems that seemed, more and more, to be spinning completely out of her control.

This was their part of the bargain: Trade first Giles, then Xander and Dawn, for the release of the Ghost of Tara. She could open the jar and it would be all done; then the remnants—and they sure were tattered—of the Scooby Gang could try to pick up and carry on.

She reached for the lid, then stopped.

Buffy had more than a big urge not to open the jar, to just tuck it back in her pocket and take it back to the Magic Box. After all, as far as she and everyone else understood it, while Giles had lifted the boundary spell on the Ghost of Tara, the no-trespassing incantation that kept Willow out was still in place. That meant that if she kept the Ghost of Tara trapped in the jar and took her back inside the shop, Willow was helpless to retrieve her.

But that hadn't stopped her from nearly killing Giles, Xander, and Dawn, had it? She'd said that, one way or another, she would find a way to get Tara's spirit back—she was so far over the line and into Revenge City that she either no longer cared about the consequences, or she truly believed she could circumvent whatever happened and ultimately get her way. And Giles, Xander, and Dawn would be helpless and unprotected out here.

Buffy stood at the counter for a long time, considering. There were so many angles here. Did she really want to keep Tara trapped? No—better to let the spirit go, either to be free forever or to return to Willow and let Willow take it from there. Willow had done her darkest, or damned near, in retaliation for the theft of Tara's spirit. If Buffy kept up her end of the bargain—despite Willow's near-failure to do so—would that *finally* be the thing that made Willow content enough to stop the destruction? To let them alone long enough to, at the very least, recover from their wounds?

She had to try it.

Buffy reached out and pulled off the jar's tight-fitting top.

There was no pause, no hesitation. If such a nebulous thing could be described in physical terms, then Tara's spirit must have been *pressing* against the top, because it burst from the narrow mouth of the jar like a shower of glitter, coating the bathroom and Buffy with sparkling silver light in an exquisite, umbrella-shaped fall. For a moment Buffy just stood there, bathed in light and warmth, and thinking that she had at least an inkling of why Willow had so wanted the Ghost of Tara back at her side. The heartbreaking thing was, that notion was immediately followed by a choking tide of grief, because if this was how Tara could make Willow feel in death, Buffy could suddenly very well imagine the devastation Willow had experienced when losing Tara in the real world.

Something smooth and warm brushed her cheek, then the sparkles coalesced into a long, thin line of light near the ceiling, almost like a flare burning in the night sky. It hovered there for maybe three seconds, then broke into a mist that flowed quickly out of sight along a crack at the edge of the windowsill that was far too small to be seen by the human eye.

And Tara was gone at last, presumably headed straight back to her beloved Willow.

Chapter Fourteen

"*Hello, Willow.*"

"Tara!" Willow gasped and whirled, then saw the Ghost of Tara not three feet away. She couldn't stop her instinctive reach for the spirit, but at the last second she pulled her hand back and let it fall to her side, before she would have to endure the heartbreak of watching her own flesh and blood pass right through Tara's body. Still, it was enough—for now—to see her love back here, with her and where she belonged. "You're here!"

"*Yes.*"

The spirit didn't say anything else, just stood there and held Willow in place with her eyes, that all-knowing gaze that had the odd effect of making Willow feel guilty and defiant at the same time. "Go ahead," Willow finally said. She could feel the blood rushing in her temples, a sure sign of stress. "I know you must have a lot to say."

The Ghost of Tara looked away for a moment, then turned her blue gaze back on Willow. *"Do I? Or do you?"*

Willow found herself grinding her teeth and forced herself to stop. "What's that supposed to mean?"

The spirit shrugged delicately. *"You have much to feel guilty about, Willow. You have much you should . . . fix."*

Willow scowled. "I refuse to feel guilty about taking whatever steps I had to so they would release you."

"They didn't hurt me." Tara's voice was so soft that Willow took an involuntary step forward as she tried to catch every word. *"They never would have, no matter what. You knew that, and yet, you . . ."* The spirit let her words trail away, let Willow's own mind fill in what she already knew.

Willow glanced away from the Ghost of Tara. "I missed you," she said softly. "Did you miss me?"

"Always. I still do."

Willow rubbed her forehead. It was a setup, and she knew it, yet she couldn't *not* ask. "What are you talking about?"

The Ghost of Tara drifted closer, and Willow tried to keep her eyes focused above the specter's neck, away from that hated, forever bloody splotch on her blouse. *"I miss the you that used to be—the one who would never hurt someone in the name of revenge, and certainly never under the guise of love, the one who would forgive."*

Willow swallowed. "That woman is gone. She died with you."

"*I don't believe that.*"

Willow sank onto a chair. "Well, you should. God knows I've proven it time and time again since your death by the things I've done." She found herself chewing on her bottom lip so hard that she was nearly drawing blood.

"*I've seen those things,*" the Ghost of Tara said. "*Firsthand. And they disappoint me more than you'll ever understand.*"

Willow gripped the arms of her chair and realized she was leaning forward. "So I can take that to mean that I also disappoint you."

"*Yes.*"

She exhaled and let herself lean back. She supposed she'd known in her soul that this was so, but to actually hear it from Tara's own ghostly lips made her feel cold all the way down to her bones. "I'm . . . sorry."

"*Then undo it.*"

Willow jerked upright again. "What?" But the Ghost of Tara said nothing, just stared at her. "Undo *what*? Warren?" Her mouth drew itself into a snarl, and her back was rigid. "Even if I could, I wouldn't. You may disagree with me, but I still believe he deserved what he got. Eye for an eye."

"*Really.*" The Ghost of Tara moved to stand in front of her so that Willow could look nowhere else but at her. "*And what did Giles, Xander, and Dawn take from you that justifies the flesh you took from them?*"

"I . . ." But really, the Ghost of Tara was right. This latest of her actions—the two Gnarls—hadn't been tit for tat, and it hadn't even been payback for the Riley golem turning on her and killing two of her coven members. The burden for that had been on the golem and therefore herself. No, the truth, the ugly, ugly truth, was that she had condemned them to being eaten alive by a demon out of nothing more than pure, blind rage. "It's too late," she said hoarsely.

"Undo it," the Ghost of Tara said again. *"Heal them."*

Willow stared at her. "No. I can't."

"You mean you won't."

A valid statement. She *could* heal them, yes. But it would take power, an immense portion of the stores she had hoarded within herself and which were meant to be used for getting Tara back. She wouldn't waste it, she *couldn't.*

"For me, Willow. Do it because I ask you to, because I cannot bear to be the reason that Giles, Xander, and Dawn die."

Willow rose from the chair, but the Ghost of Tara did not move. She either had to stand nose to nose with the spirit, or force herself to walk right through her, something she absolutely despised. "They're not dead," she said.

"But they soon will be." When Willow frowned, the Ghost of Tara continued. *"Their injuries are too severe, Willow. You went too far."* The ghost's luminescent gaze seemed to paralyze Willow. *"If you don't do something, Giles will die tonight, and Xander*

and Dawn won't make it to the end of tomorrow."

And just like that, the Ghost of Tara faded from sight.

Die?

Really *die?*

Willow stood there for a long moment, then let her suddenly weak knees bend so she could sit once more. If she was to be completely honest with herself, she'd always known the possibility was there. But had she really thought it would happen, that down-and-dirty, ashes-to-ashes, dust-to-dust result?

No.

A world without Giles in it, without Xander and Dawn. Buffy had already lost her mother, and she wasn't close with her father. Dawn was all she had left, Giles in some ways a sort of surrogate father figure. Willow thought that she shouldn't care about these things, because she had lost too—lost the one person who'd mattered the most to her, and wouldn't life without her foes constantly annoying her be so much easier?

But . . . she did care.

Could she do it? Could she repair the damage that had been done without sapping her own reserves so much that she would be unable to bring Tara back? Maybe . . . but maybe not.

"Do it because I ask you to," the Ghost of Tara had said. The spirit hadn't said she would leave, as she had said when Willow had been so angry over the destruction the Riley golem had wrought that she'd been about to kill Xander, Dawn, and Anya. That meant she had a choice in the matter. A yes vote meant she might

deplete her energy sources but that she would please Tara's spirit: always a good thing. A no meant the three of them would likely die, and their deaths would be a black mark on the eternal tablet of her soul, like Warren's. No matter what her anger wanted to make her believe, in the great final tally of things, when actions were weighed against deeds, if it came down to it, she would have no counterbalance for the deaths of Giles, Xander, and Dawn.

She didn't know where the Ghost of Tara had gone, but Willow had no doubt that she was watching as Willow quickly went through her Book of Shadows and mixed up three bags of powder. Such a tricky thing she was about to do, right in the middle of a public hospital. Not so much different from when she had pulled Warren's other bullet out of Buffy and healed her on the day Tara had died, but with three times the mojo required and, face it, a lot more body area to cover. She had healed Buffy with nothing but the power of her mind, but she'd need help with repairing the damage done to these three, a pouch of mystical healing herbs to jump-start each process and a pinch of pulverized earth and cotton fibers to show their bodies how her spell wanted the flesh to knit itself back together. And, of course, plenty of Willow's own dark and powerful essence.

Willow stepped out of the thick robe she was wearing and stood without clothes in the center of the loft for a moment, feeling the drafts raise chill bumps across her flesh and drive away some of the flush that always seemed to be present now, the constant wash of warmth borne of the bitterness of Tara's death and the resentment at all the things—Buffy and the others included—that had served to bar her from getting her lover back. The anger, the resentment, the secret fear that she wouldn't succeed—she had to leave it all here. She would need everything inside her for the coming magicks, which themselves would serve to do more than heal the injuries she had caused: They would be the first test of whether she could, by force of will and alchemy, make human flesh actually regenerate.

A wave of her hand and Willow was fully dressed in black jeans and a long-sleeved sheer black blouse beneath a black leather vest. Everything fit perfectly and comfortably, right down to her boots: two-inch heels with thick rubber bottoms that would muffle her footsteps in the hospital and, hopefully, make her less noticeable. A final glance at her Book of Shadows and she left it behind, content to rely on memory and the spell materials she'd put together.

Next stop: Sunnydale Hospital.

When Willow appeared out of nowhere, Buffy stood so quickly that the heavy chair she was sitting on over-turned.

The alarming crash it should have made never happened. Willow made some strange snapping motion in the air with one finger and the chair wobbled for a moment, then pulled back up and righted itself without a sound. Buffy had only a second or two to register the range of emotions on her companions' faces—dismay, fear, anger—then she was primed and ready for whatever fight was about to take place.

"Haven't you done enough damage?" Buffy demanded. "Or have you come to finish the job?"

Anya, who was watching Willow warily, suddenly lifted her head. "Wait—what's that?" She sniffed the air. "Adder's-tongue, comfrey, Irish moss, shepherd's purse—Buffy, she's here to try to *heal* them!"

Willow raised one eyebrow. "Always the public-announcement system, aren't you, Anya?"

"You think so?" Buffy glared at her suspiciously. "Why would she? It makes no sense."

"Why do I do anything for you people anymore?" Willow retorted. Her gaze was glacial, black as an unlit coal mine. "Because Tara asked me to, you fools." She gave a mirthless chuckle. "You really should thank her, you know. If it wasn't for her, you, Anya, and the rest of your little gang would have been dead back when my cat-demon was alive, and Spike and Oz would still be my personal petting zoo."

"Oh, and did *I* say thanks?" There was no mistaking the quiet venom in Oz's voice.

Willow was unaffected. "You don't look any worse for the wear," she pointed out. "And Spike seems to have even regained some semblance of his centuries-dead brain."

Spike sat up. "Hey, no need to get all personal about things, love!"

Willow ignored him and looked at Buffy instead. "Just remember, what I do here tonight is for Tara. Not for Giles or for any of the others—and definitely not for *you*."

Buffy's mouth opened as Willow started to walk away, but for a moment she didn't know what she wanted to say. Her baby sister was lying across the hall in the intensive care ward, near death and probably scarred for life if she did survive, and Buffy would be damned before she'd mouth the words "thank you" to Willow for fixing this when the damage had been caused by her in the first place. But there were other things on her mind too, important things, and when the words came out of her mouth, she was just as surprised as the rest of them at what she said. "Why do we have to be enemies, Willow?"

Willow stopped with her back to Buffy and the others, and she didn't turn around when she spoke. "We don't, Buffy. And we aren't—not anymore. Tara asked me to undo this, and so for her, I will. After that, I don't have time for you anymore. As of tonight, we aren't enemies. We aren't friends. We aren't *anything.*" Her head turned, and she raked all of them with that same, obsidian gaze. "Not anything at all, ever again."

And Buffy, Anya, Oz, and Spike stared after Willow as she crossed the hall and pushed through the doors into the intensive care area.

It was all so different.

It was something she'd taken for granted, but Willow supposed there was quite a bit of cushion in torturing someone in a nice, dark cave—one with a dirt floor to soak up the blood and stone, and earthen walls to absorb the moans and screams. There were no such luxuries here, even if that was a strange term to use for it. Oh no, this was the modern-day world, with the next best thing to bright sunlight spilling from the light fixtures overhead; clean white walls; pale gray linoleum; and sterile white sheets and bandages that contrasted screamingly with bloodstains. The only thing around to block sound waves were the separator curtains, and every one of those was wide open to make sure all the nurses and doctors—at least a half dozen—could have uninterrupted visual access to anyone's monitors at any time. Heart, blood pressure, oxygen, respiration, you name it—there was a beeping, blinking, musical machine for every one of those, plus a few more Willow had never known existed.

Maybe it was the fact that she'd been gutsy enough to simply waltz right through the front door that did it, but she got almost all the way down to the far end and the nurses' station closest to where Giles, Xander, and Dawn had been placed before anyone noticed her.

"You—stop right there! You're not supposed to be in here!" The voice was sharp and all business, no screwing around here. When Willow turned, she saw an extremely pretty young nurse with chin-length brown hair striding toward her. "This is a sterile environment," she snapped. "Visitors can't walk right in!"

"Shhhhh," Willow said, and held her forefinger to her lips, effectively cutting off whatever else the young woman was going to say. Her throat worked and her lips moved, but no sound came out; one hand flew to her throat, then, surprisingly, she scowled and looked quickly around. Willow had to admire the nurse. She was smart and was *not* prone to panicking, and if she couldn't raise the alarm vocally, she was damned well going to find another way to do it. Before she could do something disastrous like get someone else's attention or, God forbid, even pull the fire alarm, Willow decided the best course of action would be to just freeze everyone in the room who was mobile.

Done.

She couldn't hold it for long, of course—there were a lot of people in there, and it took too much concentration away from the thing that had to take priority here, the healing. The monitors were still bleeping monotonously, and she could take a little bit of comfort in that: If one of them went wonky, she'd have to let go of the staff and hightail it out of the IC ward, and come back for another try when things calmed down. And according to the Ghost of Tara, she didn't have that kind of time to spare, because if she didn't step in, Giles was going to head to the great beyond sometime in the next several hours.

Looking down at the three of them, Willow had to admit that she felt a certain . . . distance from it all. Had she really done this? No, of course not—it had been the Gnarls, not her. Wait—she *had* done it, because she was the one who had come up with the idea of doing it, and who'd specifically whizbanged those two demons into existence and given them their free dinners. Yes, she *was* to blame for this, and no matter what her reasons had been at the time, with the Ghost of Tara safely back at the loft, and nothing left—not really—to be angry about, it suddenly seemed like they'd paid a really huge price for a very small offense.

Giles looked old and gray and bled out, as though he was only two or three steps away from already being a corpse. She had never seen him looking like this, so weak and vulnerable, so far *gone*. A glance to the right showed her that, like Xander, Giles's sheet had been folded down to his hips so that no weight rested on the huge, open wound across his stomach; Dawn's sheet rested across her chest, barely a half inch from the long strips of missing flesh that went horizontally across her body from shoulder to shoulder. Xander's and Dawn's coloring was a little better than Giles's, but Willow could see the tinges of gray— death—creeping in at the edges; by dawn tomorrow they would look like Giles did now, and Giles's sheet would be over his face.

The medical staff had dressed their wounds with some sort of clear mesh, nonstick bandage treated with about a pound each of something that was probably antibiotic ointment. Willow clenched her teeth and hoped to God their pain medication would keep them knocked out long enough for her to begin the ritual . . . which meant her peeling away the protective bandaging on all three.

She needn't have worried—although she winced when the dressings wanted to cling to the wounds, not a one of the three seemed to feel anything as Willow passed her hand over each and the gore-soaked coverings finally let go and rose in the air. She spun them off to the side and dropped them in one of the wastebaskets, then swallowed, appalled and intimidated in spite of herself as she looked at the Gnarls' handiwork.

She'd never seen anything that looked like this outside of a meat package in the grocery store freezer, or maybe during a dissection course in high school biology.

She pulled the three pouches from her pocket and tugged at the ribbons that closed each, letting them fall to the floor as she tried to reassure herself. She'd done this before, with Buffy on the operating table, had pulled Warren's bullet right out of the Slayer and fixed her then and there. Sure, this was three times the work and the wounds were a lot bigger, but she was confident. Besides, now she had three times the material, and a whole lot more mojo to back her up, right? So one packet for each, and—

The bleep on Giles's heart monitor faltered.

Willow stared at it, vaguely aware that she was holding her breath.

bleepbleepbleep

Gone was the regular, slow rhythm that in just two minutes she'd so come to take for granted.

bleepbleep . . . bleepbleepbleep

Now it was erratic and fast, with unpredictable pauses thrown in that went long enough to make her own pulse race. Jesus, she hadn't realized it might happen so fast—

bleep . . .

. . .

. . . bleep

Now! Willow thought very clearly. *I have to do this NOW!*

Heart hammering, she yanked on the neck of the first pouch and nearly dropped it, finally managed to

get it open and fling its contents into the air above
Giles's stomach. There wasn't time for fancy rhymes
or flashy magick moves. "Angita, hear my invoca-
tion!" she cried. She raced to Xander's side and did
the same with the second pouch, then repeated the
motion with the last one across Dawn's chest. "I ask
that you repair the damage done to these three by dark
forces. In the name of your own divine healing powers, make it so!"

bl . . .

 . . .

 . . .

Willow's hand shot to her mouth as Giles's monitor
stuttered and went completely, utterly silent, then went
suddenly into a nerve-shattering shrieking alarm. She
could see her healing powders swirling madly over the
wounds of each of them, changing colors from red to
flesh tone and back again as it worked to re-create and
re-knit the missing skin. But Giles was the most griev-
ously injured—had she come too late to save him?

. . . ep bleep bleep bleep

Willow's lungs let out air in a rush, leaving her
feeling light-headed and weak. As the powder clouds
abruptly finished their tasks, each sifted down to
land in a thick layer of gray-white ash across newly
made flesh that was angry pink and tender looking,
like a bad sunburn. Suddenly there was noise all
around Willow—that nasty little surprise with Giles's
heart monitor had made her lose her hold on the
freeze, and now that nurse was snapping at someone
to call security while another one appeared right in

front of her, demanding that Willow tell her what the hell she'd thrown on those three patients.

Willow looked at the two angry faces, then glanced over for a final check of Giles, Xander, and Dawn. They'd be sore when they woke up, but as a triple project went, this one was pretty successful. Not a one of them was even going to have a scar. And as for all the doctors and nurses yammering at one another and pointing at her and just generally freaking out in every direction—

A well-powered Wiccan just had to appreciate the ability to teleport.

Chapter Fifteen

It was good to be back at the Magic Box again. Even so, walking around the shop, touching the trinkets on the shelves and running his hand over the spines of the books, Giles couldn't help wonder how many more times he could stand being nearly killed. He supposed he would do what he must to follow his destiny.

It was just that he was so . . . *tired*. This time, his second near-death experience since Warren had killed Tara, had really opened his eyes—or closed them, if he wanted to be facetious about his phrasing. Both of those times had been at Willow's hand. In the realm of all things possible, it had never occurred to him that Willow might turn out *this* way, that she would walk away from the people who loved her most and would even *hurt* them. Her reasons mattered, yes, but they weren't the point, and they weren't *good* enough—

everyone encounters difficulties along the path of his or her life, people and situations that dump everything on its head. The trick isn't so much in how you deal with the situation but in how you come *out* of it afterward, and therein was the core of it: Whatever you do to deal, you always keep an eye on where you are going. If Willow had done that lately, surely she saw that the road ahead led to a place in which she might not want to end up.

Giles felt the skin across his stomach burn where the waistband of his slacks pushed against the bandage the hospital had wrapped around him. While they were at a loss to explain the healing, it certainly wasn't the first time something strange had happened in that hospital—after all, this was Sunnydale. They'd traded the antibiotic ointment for, of all things, cocoa butter; the healed skin was as new and soft as an infant's, and he and the others were to use the tasty-smelling stuff as a heavy moisturizer until they were sure the newly formed flesh wasn't going to peel.

Newly formed flesh . . . what she had taken away, Willow had also restored.

Buffy had taken Dawn home to rest, but he and the others had gotten the full story at the hospital, right after Willow had winked herself out of the intensive care ward and left it in chaos. To do that had shown an utter disregard for possible consequences, but at the same time, what else *could* she have done? She certainly couldn't have explained it, so why suffer the fallout?

So Willow had healed them because Tara had

asked her to, not because she had regretted her actions. That made it a bittersweet victory. He would have much preferred it to be the other way around: Willow healing them because she was sorry. But she wasn't, and Giles was afraid she wasn't ever going to be, and he didn't know what he could do about that. This was a Willow he'd never dreamed existed—at least when he'd been subjected to the tortures visited upon him by Angelus, he could explain it. It hadn't made it any easier for Giles to accept Angel when he'd gotten his soul back, but at least he could understand it.

But what he *could* do, if he backtracked on the steps he'd taken and did some very careful research, was undo a wrong that he himself had done.

Moving slowly, Giles started a pot of water to make a cup of good strong English tea, then went to pull out the timeworn books he was going to need to make this work.

Xander had never thought he would be so grateful to be staring up at his own ceiling.

For most of his life he'd been one of those people who could drop off to sleep at the flip of a light switch—it went out, and so did he. That luxury had disappeared the day he'd begun having doubts about marrying Anya, and abandoning her at the altar had seemed to solidify this unwanted change in his body clock. He still loved her desperately, but nothing he said could make her understand that he had done what he had done for her own good, for her *happiness*. For Anya, it was only the here and now, the pain and humiliation, and the future for the two of them that was now lost forever. It wasn't hard to comprehend: She'd lived a thousand years and had her demonness stripped away, then thought that she could at least spend her limited life span as a mortal with him, in love. To her mind, time was short and precious and needed to be lived to its fullest, and Xander had taken the potential clean out of that new future.

And here he was, eyes wide open again—but this time, for different reasons entirely.

Willow tried to kill me.

That was a bad enough line to be rampaging around his overloaded brain, but apparently it wasn't high enough on the self-torment scale. Everytime it popped into his thoughts, it was followed immediately by—

Willow WANTED to kill me.

Tried to, wanted to, nearly *did.*

That at the end she had also healed him rather than let him die didn't matter. Some things might be forgiven but were never forgotten, and this latest of his misadventures at the hands of Wicked Willow was holding the top slot on his newly forming nonforgivable list. It was like the employee who made off with the weekly payroll, then returned it to the company and said, "I'm sorry." What rational person really expected the boss to forgive and forget? The return might keep the guy out of jail—and even that was a long shot—but it damned sure wasn't going to land him back on the employee roster or standing in line for the next Employee of the Month award.

After getting him settled in and making sure he had food, Anya had reluctantly gone back to her apartment, too afraid to sleep over because of the super-sensitive skin on his stomach. Xander felt like a kid who'd washed away his mondo-SPF sunblock in the pool, then ignorantly stayed outside for four hours. Even though the outside looked like it was healed, the slightest touch across his belly was like a ripple of fire. His pajama bottoms, for instance, easily could have doubled as a belt of live coals. Finally he cranked up the thermostat and stripped down to just himself and a sheet across his hips.

And hours later, Xander still lay with his eyes wide open in the darkness, trying desperately to understand why everything in the world had gone so terribly, terribly wrong.

What is Willow thinking right now?

Buffy sat on a chair next to Dawn's bed, content—for now—to watch her little sister sleep. She felt so . . . *sad* for Dawn, to be so young and normal, so human—no matter what anyone said—and have to endure that much pain. Sure, Xander and Giles had gone through the same thing, with Giles getting the worst of it, but they were older, more prepared. She wasn't positive—she wasn't stupid enough to think that her little sister had told her *everything*—but this might be Dawn's first encounter with something this vicious, and because that something had turned out to be someone who'd once been a friend, it just made it that much more awful. Dawn had already ended up with a broken arm because of Willow's former magick addiction. Buffy had no idea how Dawn was going to feel about Willow when this was all over. A broken arm actually seemed kind of tame compared with the expanse of beet-red skin across Dawn's collarbone and the agony she'd gone through.

Buffy scrubbed at her face with her hands. She wished she could understand *why*. She was so angry that she just wanted to beat Willow senseless, grind her into the ground until she understood just how much pain her victims had gone through. Was *that* what Willow was feeling—that sense of "I'm going through this, so everyone else should too"? When times were at their worst and her own responsibilities had gotten too heavy to bear, hadn't Buffy wished that same thing: that other people knew exactly what she was going through?

Sure, but the truth of it was that no one ever *would*. Everyone had their own problems, their own brand of pain—Sunnydale was like the world's greatest Pain-Mart. Giles dealt with the Council's rejection of his lifelong destiny; Dawn struggled against the idea that she wasn't even real; Xander was haunted by his inability to let himself commit to Anya; and Anya herself had endured a woman's worst nightmare and heartache. As for herself, Buffy had to live with the knowledge that, except when the Universe had twisted a little and given them Faith, she was different from every single person she would ever meet—

One girl in all the world, to find them where they gather. . . .

No one would ever understand how she felt. Willow thought that because of Tara's death she was alone now, and in a way, that was true. Buffy had lost in love twice herself, but for different reasons; Giles had lost Jenny Calendar at the hands of Angelus, but he had been at the beginning of falling in love, and that meant his loss wasn't like Willow's, where she and Tara had just mended their heart-shattering breakup. It wasn't less important, less substantial . . . just *different*.

No, she couldn't understand this. In all the pain she had endured, or Giles had endured, or Anya or Xander or Dawn, not a one of them had ever wished that misery or hurt on someone else, and to be honest, Buffy couldn't imagine Willow—even the new, down-and-dirty version—doing that. There seemed to be no explanation other than they had simply gotten in Willow's way.

And that was just an unacceptable reason to justify the things Willow had done. Sooner or later, Buffy would find a way to make Willow pay.

In the darkest part of night, when the moon above Sunnydale had dropped low behind the tallest trees and the sun had not yet come up, Giles was finally ready to bring back the last two of the women he'd removed from Willow's coven. He'd used a scattering spell, but something had gone wrong and it had turned into a banishing incantation. Banishment and scattering were supposed to be two different things, with banishment more a punishment for wrongdoing. He'd had no proof of any such thing, but perhaps his choice of words—he dimly recalled labeling the women as a "group of hell" and using the phrase "their own dark deeds"—had negated the scattering part by putting an assumption into the magick that he had never intended. As a result, several of the women had gone through hell, and for this he would always feel ashamed. He couldn't bear to think that the missing two were enduring the same torment.

At least this time there was no hellish cat-beast to battle or avoid, and Willow was nowhere around to interfere. He didn't know what she was doing now that she'd had the Ghost of Tara returned to her, but he would deal with that later. Oddly, he felt no animosity toward her—at least not on the part of himself. For Xander and Dawn . . . well, that was another story. Xander was a big boy, and yes, they would all heal. But Dawn . . . she was a teenager, an innocent. To put her through this and essentially teach her that someone she'd once trusted would try to *kill* her . . . that was nearly unforgivable. He'd forgiven a lot of things from a lot of people since Buffy had come into his life, but this . . . this might be the one thing he could not. Time was the only thing that would tell if there was still a place in his heart for the woman Willow had become.

Speaking of Willow, Giles had no idea how she'd managed to bring back the women to begin with. Obviously, he couldn't just give her a ring and ask, so he was going to have to improvise on his own and see what happened. He'd come up with a modern-day map of the world and spread it out on the floor, and now he placed five black candles around it at evenly spaced intervals. As Anya had pointed out in both her attempts at getting him to walk again, black was actually a good color, particularly if the spell caster wanted to repel negative energy. God knew they'd had enough of that around here and Giles didn't want any more; he was also hoping he could avoid bringing anything . . . *unwanted* back with them—provided he succeeded in bringing them back at all—whether it was bad emotions, bad physical ramifications, or actual undesirable creatures.

With the candles burning around the map, he poured a tiny pile of ground mint, holly, and thyme on the spot in California where Sunnydale was. On top of this he carefully positioned a polished Adventurine, the metallic-looking stone that is sometimes called Indian Jade. This particular stone was red, and was supposed to turn a person's luck in the right direction. He placed it here in the hopes that the women he was seeking would be able to find their way home. Finally, because he had no idea what the two missing Wiccans looked like, to represent them Giles cut two one-inch-tall pieces of white paper that vaguely resembled paper dolls.

With the candles burning and no one else around but himself, Giles took a deep breath and continued trying to set right the thing he'd done wrong.

Chapter Sixteen

"*You have visitors.*"

Willow blinked and opened her eyes, then squinted up at the Ghost of Tara. "What?"

"*You have visitors,*" the spirit repeated. "*Outside.*"

Willow frowned and looked down at the book on her lap, then around at the darkened loft. She'd been reading up on the final phase of what she believed she was going to have to do to resurrect Tara, and she must have fallen asleep. No one else was around, which meant it had to be nearly sunrise. The women always left just before then, and a glance at the nearest window backed that up. No light outside yet, but the air had that particular predawn quality to it, that odd sense of heaviness and snap. They must have seen her sleeping and left without waking her. She wouldn't admit it to any of them, but she was . . . well, exhausted. The devastation of Tara's death, the constant up-and-down stress since then—it was taking its toll. Sometimes it felt like she was fighting the entire Universe—destiny, Buffy and Giles, time itself—and she was just so *tired* of the struggle. Now she just wanted to bring Tara back to life and step out of it all, live the normal life they should have had. Not even that—she wanted a life free of the supernatural and vampires and magick and maniacs who wanted to kill the people around her.

The Ghost of Tara was still standing there, waiting, and Willow glanced at her, then at the window, finally pushing herself up and wandering over to stare out the glass. The spirit was right: There were people down there. Who—

Oh, great.

She started to turn away and stalk back to her chair, then Willow found herself again face-to-face with the Ghost of Tara.

"They have things to say," the spirit said. *"It's important you listen."*

Willow sighed. "I don't have any *answers* for them!" She spun and glared out the window, as if doing so would make the small group of people gathered on the sidewalk below disappear. "What do you want me to do, bounce down there, flip my hand, and say, 'Sorry! They got sucked away in a spell, and I have no idea where they went or how to bring them back! Too bad, so sad!'?" Her eyes narrowed. "Hey, maybe I'll send them over to talk to Giles. Let *him* explain where he sent them."

The Ghost of Tara said nothing, just watched her

with those luminous, liquid-looking blue eyes. Waiting. Expecting.

"Tara, I don't know what to *tell* them," Willow repeated helplessly.

"You can't just leave them down there," the spirit said calmly.

"Why not?" Willow folded her arms, vaguely aware that she sounded like a petulant little girl. "It's not like they can get in."

The Ghost of Tara tilted her head. *"Open the window and listen."*

Willow pressed her lips together impatiently, then did what Tara had instructed, pushing up the window enough to hear but careful to keep the illusion to her visitors that there were no windows in the building. The sound carried well in the predawn darkness, and she had no trouble hearing what was said and who was saying it.

"What do you mean there's no door? Of course there's a door—every place has to have a door!" said Brenda, Megan's mother, her voice elevated by indignation.

"I'm telling you, not this building," said Megan's father. *"And look up—no windows, either."*

"Oh, there's a door and windows, all right," said Megan's grandmother. *"You just can't see them."*

"Oh, here we go again with the abracadabra baloney," Brenda said sarcastically. *"I can always wave my arms and say, 'Open sesame!'"*

"I'll tell you what," Megan's father said. Something about the tone of his voice had changed, as if

he'd made up his mind about something. *"I've had just about enough of this. Give me your cell phone, Brenda. I'm calling the cops."*

"I don't know what you expect them *to do about anything,"* the grandmother retorted.

Upstairs, Willow swallowed but tried to look unconcerned. "Exactly," she said to the Ghost of Tara. "They can't do anything."

"Is that what you think?" A corner of the spirit's mouth turned down. *"The world does not entirely exist in the magickal, Willow. As powerful as you are, you cannot fight everyone all the time. There will always be more people in authority in the realm of the normal than you, always someone questioning what you do, demanding explanations for the questionable things you've done. Would you have attention called to those things so that you are under constant scrutiny?"*

Willow opened her mouth, then shut it again. The Ghost of Tara was right. The Sunnydale Police might never be able to hold her in a jail cell, but they could certainly make her life miserable. If Megan's mother and father accused her of kidnapping their daughter, the cops would watch her 24/7, and they would do it for months—maybe even years. No, she had to smooth this over somehow, stall them until she could figure out what she could do—if anything at all—to fix this. "All right," she said finally. "I'll talk to them."

"Quickly."

Willow swallowed, then glanced down at the sidewalk again. Megan's father was talking animatedly on a cell phone, gesturing in the air to emphasize his words. Marvelous—he'd already gotten the police on the line. Willow brought her thumb and forefinger together in a circle, then flicked them apart, abruptly breaking his connection. The man on the sidewalk stopped in mid-sentence, then scowled at the phone, shook it, and held it to his ear. When he realized it was still dead, he thrust it angrily at Megan's mother, then glared up at Willow's building again.

Willow rubbed the sleep from her eyes, then went into teleport mode. It was time to face the music.

Things were going better than expected.

Giles had a pretty good wind going inside the Magic Box, and there were two spots of dark energy swirling above points on the map that he felt fairly confident identified the locations of the last two Wiccans he'd banished. The spots reminded him of ominous-looking twirling black marbles. Giles didn't know the women's names, but he didn't need that to bring them back. What he *did* need was a whole lot of luck and for the Universe to look on his actions with a more than generous dose of sympathy. This was so far afield of what he'd ever thought he'd be doing—bringing someone he'd banished *back* from God knew where—that he felt like he was trying to tread water with metal weights tied around his ankles. He had no idea what he was going to do if they came back injured or angry, or worse. He just knew he had to try.

The candles were lit, the room was primed. Now all Giles could do was hope that whatever entity was important was actually going to *listen.* He took a deep breath, then launched into the short returning spell he'd put together.

"Reverse tonight that spell of mine," he intoned, "that sent those women far and wide. Return the last of those taken away." The spots of whirling black increased their rotation and were suddenly shot through with little lines of red, like tiny zaps of internal lighting. Moving quickly, Giles touched one of the two tiny paper dolls to each swirling circle of black and crimson. Both caught fire instantly, and he brought them together and dropped them on top of the pile of herbs that covered the spot on the map that represented Sunnydale. "Bring them now to their rightful place, with memories not of these past events!"

Often when Giles performed a spell that was a bit more involved than a simple, instant command, nothing happened right away. There was an infuriating pause, usually just long enough to make him question whether he'd been successful at it. Not this time. Perhaps force of will or desire on the part of the two women had something to do with it, because the two madly turning spots of ebony zipped through the air above the map and crashed together over the pile of ground herbs and ash. When they hit, they ignited into a single, bright flash, strong enough to make Giles instinctively step back and leave him with spots dancing in front of his eyes. The ball of light trembled for a second, then dropped flat onto the Sunnydale spot and enveloped it before extinguishing just as quickly as it had lit up.

Giles blinked until his vision cleared, then peered

at the map on the table. There was a hole about the size of a quarter burned in it, and nothing was left of the herbs or the paper. Had the women made it back? He stared anxiously around the room, but if they had, the Magic Box certainly hadn't been their destination. It was as dark and quiet in there as when he'd first set up to do the spell; the only difference was the faintest smell of toasted herbs and singed paper.

He'd done all he could to bring them back. All that was left was to wait and see where . . . and *if* . . . they showed up.

"I told you," Drake, Megan's father, said as he stared at Willow, "that you had two days or I would call the police. Well, I meant it." He held up his cell phone for her to see. "They're on their way here now." He looked less tall than he had when Willow had seen him previously, as though the weight of not being able to find his daughter was finally beating him down.

Grandma had come with him, of course, as had his wife. Before Willow could answer to Drake, Grandma jabbed a wrinkled finger in her direction, but it, too, had less of the energy she'd shown on her previous visit. Was it for the same reason: that they'd been so convinced that threatening Willow would fix everything and return their precious Megan? Although it clearly hadn't worked, her voice was still vehement. "I know you're the one who cut off his cell phone too," she said triumphantly. "But you weren't in time, you know. He'd already given them the address."

Had it really been two days? *Only* two days? With

the Gnarls and everything else that had happened, it seemed like weeks had passed. Maybe to these people, weeks *had* passed. Willow knew from personal experience that when you spent your days waiting for the return of someone you desperately loved, each hour seemed like a day, and each day like a year. "Look," Willow said with exaggerated patience, "I already explained to you that I don't know where Megan is. I haven't seen her—"

"You're lying," Brenda, Megan's mother, put in. "I can always tell when a person is lying. It's the way their eyes shift to the left, and yours are practically poking out of that side of your head."

"I'm *not* lying," Willow insisted. "I haven't seen her in a long time."

"Then where did she go?" Brenda demanded. "Just tell me that and we'll leave."

Willow spread her hands. "I don't know," she said honestly. "I really don't. If I did, I'd go and get her, just to make you happy!"

"If you don't know where their daughter is, perhaps you know where my niece is," said a new voice from behind her. "Her name is Dilek."

Willow spun, then gaped at the police officer who stood there with his hands on his hips—she hadn't even heard the cruiser pull up to the curb behind her. There was a gold nameplate on one of his shirt pockets that read KOVARY, but the name meant nothing to Willow. Besides Amy, she'd never known or cared to know the full name of any of her Wiccans. Officer Kovary was tall and slender, with thick salt-and-pepper hair and a no-nonsense expression along with black eyes that held absolutely no warmth or forgiveness.

"I talked to her friends," he continued as he pulled a small notebook from a back pocket and flipped it open. "And when she didn't come home, I searched her room top to bottom." He began ticking off points on his paper with a ballpoint pen. "I admit that I don't believe in half of this stuff, but I *will* check into every aspect of it if that's what it takes to find her." He jabbed the pen at the paper. "Wiccan rituals, a coven, spells, and all that nonsense. I never saw any indication that she was into that goth stuff, but a lot of kids hide things pretty well." His gaze bored into Willow's. "See, my sister and her husband were killed in a car wreck when Dilek was four, and I've taken care of her ever since. I *won't* lose my niece like I lost my sister: One day they're alive, the next they're just . . . gone." He scanned Megan's family. "And I guarantee you that you won't get rid of me as easily as you might someone who isn't wearing a uniform."

Now Willow was completely at a loss about what to say. The honest-to-God truth was that she really *didn't* know where either of these young women were, but that was never going to fly here. She'd been told that Njeri had had no family, no one to mourn or miss her passing, and Flo had found a way of her own to deal with Anan's family. Anan had always been the wild one in her family's eyes, and sadly, they'd believed Flo's tale about Anan heading off to New York City to find better opportunities. Depressingly, Anan's mom and dad had been nothing more than critical—even calling their daughter a fool. Would they change their tone if they knew she was dead? Only Flo—and, to a point, Willow—knew or mourned Anan's loss.

But Megan and Dilek . . . with the Sunnydale Police Department coming down on her, too many things could unravel—yeah, she could teleport when and where she wanted, but what would that really accomplish? She'd be Bonnie in the Wiccan equivalent of Bonnie and Clyde, always on the run, trying to get to her stuff and find a way to do her Tara resurrection spell without having it destroyed by interruptions or distractions. Next to these people—and possibly Megan and Dilek themselves—no one wanted them back here more than Willow. In fact—

"It's all right, Uncle Jim. I'm right here."

Willow couldn't suppress a gasp as Officer Kovary whirled to the left and saw his niece. For a moment—a very *short* moment—there was silence as the other three people stared at the other young woman now standing beside them: Megan. Then everyone started jabbering and shrieking at once.

"Oh my *God*!" Brenda screeched at her daughter. "We were so worried. Where have you *been*?"

"Are you all right?" the grandmother demanded, shooting Willow a damning look. "Did she hurt you in some way? Don't you dare be afraid to tell us the truth, because she can't do *anything* to you with all of us here, and you know of course that you're never going to be around her again—"

"You've got some explaining to do," Officer Kovary told his niece sternly. "I've been worried sick, practically scouring this town with a toothbrush. Then I heard the call tonight come in and decided to answer it myself."

But Dilek only gave her uncle a blank stare. "Call? Call about what?"

The policeman glanced sideways at Drake. "Well, we lost the connection, but the caller said something about a kidnapping at this address."

Megan turned to frown at her father. "Oh, Dad—please tell me you didn't do that. How embarrassing."

"You've been gone for *weeks*," Drake said defensively. "This was the last place you'd been hanging around. What were we supposed to think?"

"That I'm in my twenties now, and not the high school girl who has to check in before midnight every night," she shot back.

"Ditto," said Dilek, earning herself a glare from her uncle.

"I'll be going now," Willow said to no one in particular. "Give everyone a chance to have your reunions and happy sappy family stuff." Her instinctive thought was to just teleport out of the whole mess, but a quick glance told her that Officer Kovary was still watching her out of the corner of his eye. Damn. Right now she was still so shell-shocked at Megan's and Dilek's sudden appearance that her mind wasn't working fast enough to come up with anything snappy or clever enough to give herself a quick exit.

To make matters worse, the policeman stepped

away from Dilek and gave her a full-on glare. "I'll tell you what, Miss Rosenberg—that's right, I know all about you, more than you probably realize. I'm going to be keeping an eye on you in the future, just to ensure that there are no more . . . *unexplained* absences like this. You—"

"Uncle Jim, stop it," Dilek interrupted. "You're making so much more out of this than is necessary."

"Then tell me where you were."

All eyes turned toward Dilek, including Megan's. Willow was careful to keep her expression neutral, but she was startled all over again at the dismayed look on Dilek's face—Willow didn't know where Dilek had been, but she'd figured the two young women hadn't been together. What she hadn't considered was that they might not remember where they'd been, and it was becoming more and more obvious that that was exactly the case. She watched and waited along with everyone else, but noticed more: like the fact that their clothes were not only clean, they looked literally brand-new, as if they'd been somehow "supplied" with their reappearance.

Dilek blinked, then blinked again under the stares leveled in her direction. "It's . . . complicated," she finally said. "And to be honest, I really don't want to go into it."

Megan stepped up next to her. For a moment, her gaze caught Willow's, but she frowned and looked away as if she wasn't sure if she should be angry or not. "Me neither," she said firmly. "I think we'd both rather just move on."

Officer Kovary fixed her with his coal-black gaze. "So the two of you were together."

Dilek looked as though she didn't know what to say, but Megan only shrugged. "It doesn't matter. We're home now, and that's what counts, isn't it?"

"Mostly," Megan's grandmother said. She reached out and snagged her granddaughter's arm, holding on to it like it was a fencepost in a hurricane.

By now, Willow had backed up until she could feel the side of the building behind her. Two more steps would put her around the corner and out of their view.

One—

Two—

"Hey, where'd that woman go?" Brenda demanded. "She still has some explaining to do!"

But Willow had already shimmered out of sight and was listening from the relative safety of the invisible upstairs window.

The group milled around for a bit on the sidewalk below, looking crankily at the building and arguing among themselves about "what to do" about Willow, as if they could really do anything at all. They couldn't see her, of course, but Willow sat at the windowsill and listened, relieved as the interest in her died out and was overshadowed by the return of the two young women. Willow saw both Megan and Dilek glance upward a couple of times—they knew she was watching and listening, and were probably wondering if she wanted them to return to her. She didn't; while they might not remember their ordeals, she was willing to bet things hadn't been all roses and honey. The last thing she wanted to do was take a chance on doing something that might trigger memories of experiences best left forgotten.

So what *had* brought about their return? Giles, of course—he must have done it. Such a good little ex-Watcher, still soaking in his overdeveloped conscience. Eye for an eye, and all Golden Rulely. Had the positions been reversed, Willow doubted she would have been so generous. Yes, she had healed him and Dawn and Xander, but she had been the catalyst for their brutal injuries and near death. Where was it written that he must repay her for undoing the damage she'd done to begin with? Especially given that the only reason she'd done so was because Tara had asked her to. It was always because of Tara.

A check out the window told her that the visitors were finally leaving. The last to file down the sidewalk was the police officer, Kovary, and he gave her—or at least the building—a look that could only be described as venomous, but at least he was going, going, and finally gone out of her life. And with his niece returned, hopefully for good.

"All's well that ends well?"

Willow turned to look back at the Ghost of Tara. "It's not ended," she said. "Not yet."

The spirit shook her head. *"And it won't,"* she pointed out. *"Not the way you want."*

Willow squeezed her eyes shut, but closing her eyelids, fragile bits of vein-crossed flesh, could do nothing to shut out the image she wanted to escape: the Ghost of Tara, standing there in a blood-soaked blouse.

"Must we have this conversation again? I feel like I'm listening to a scratchy old LP with a record player needle stuck in its groove."

"I'm only trying to spare you the disappointment that's bound to happen."

Willow opened her eyes, trying to force her gaze to stay above the spirit's neck. "I'm thinking there's a source of power I haven't tapped."

The Ghost of Tara's blue eyes never wavered. *"Giles doesn't have enough power to give you, Willow. No one has enough."*

Willow shivered a little and hugged herself. "My bad. I meant to say *help*. Look what he was able to do for Megan and Dilek, even when I couldn't find them."

"The creator of an incantation always has the most power over it," Tara reminded her. *"Because he does not believe in his heart that what you want to do is right, his involvement will hurt you more than help."*

Willow was silent as she thought about this. The Ghost of Tara was right, of course. It didn't take a Norman Vincent Peale graduate to know that if a person didn't believe in something fully, especially when he was dealing in the realm of the magickal, the only result was going to be failure.

"Fine," Willow said eventually. "Then I'll just do what I'd intended all along.

"I'll take care of it by myself."

Chapter Seventeen

There were times when Willow felt like the days and weeks moved past as quickly as sap trickling down the side of a tree in the middle of a frigid winter. As a counterbalance, there seemed to be plenty of other times that zipped by so quickly, she barely had time to breathe or firmly record them in her memory. It was those times that felt like they'd happened to a stranger, that she'd been somehow standing outside herself and watching the whole thing unfold.

Bringing Buffy back to life was a perfect example of that.

Willow sat alone at her table and went over her spell books and all the research volumes she'd gathered. Her coven was going to return tonight to pick up the ingredients they needed, then they would all assemble at Tara's grave for the final spell. This was it—Willow had to be ready, had to bring the endless researching and power-grubbing to its intended conclusion. She'd told them this earlier and had seen the relief in their eyes, plus the greed in Amy's as she realized the promise that Willow had dangled to get her to cooperate—that of being the most powerful Wiccan in Sunnydale when Willow was out of the biz—was almost within her grasp. There was, Willow knew, infighting and squabbling going on among the Wiccans, a jockeying for position beneath the up-and-coming Amy. It was petty and ugly and tacky, and Willow wanted no part of it; once she had her precious Tara back, for all she cared, they could backstab and catclaw one another to death.

Speaking of death, the start of that Buffy spell had been, Willow thought, the first time she'd committed murder.

It was just a deer, she told herself now, but even after all this time, the guilt was there, and the memory—how convenient that the worst part of it should so suddenly come back to her—of the small, spotted fawn's trusting, liquid brown eyes as they'd looked into hers, its clean-smelling, velvet-soft fur beneath her fingers as she'd stroked its head and back. Drawn by the soothing words of her spell and the earthy, alluring smell of the herbs she'd sprinkled in the clearing, the tiny animal had truly never realized the danger.

Her knife, wickedly sharp, flashing downward and sinking through the creature's skin and deep into its body, practically without any effort at all.

So much blood from such a small animal. The

scarlet life fluid had gone everywhere, covering the front of Willow's blouse and her hands as she managed to fill the vial with as much as she needed, then sprinkled the fawn with the rest of the mixture she'd made up and softly spoken a thank-you to the gods who had so generously offered up a portion of themselves at her request. Even back then she'd found herself sitting and staring at her handiwork, wishing she could somehow bring this infant deer back to life and get what she needed somewhere else. It wasn't possible, of course. Killing something, or *someone,* was the one irredeemable act. There was no chance to look down at the body and say, "Oh, hey—sorry about that. I didn't mean to kill you, so could you just get up again and go on about your business?" How much easier life would be if such a thing were possible.

Of course, even if it was, a person would have to *want* to undo the bad. A person would have to have a *conscience.*

Would Warren have wanted to change what had happened? Willow didn't know. In fact, she didn't *care.* The down and dirty of it was that it was done, there had been retribution, and it was time to move on from there. And the moving on included a special kind of undoing, something that only a special kind of Wiccan—a very *powerful* Wiccan—could accomplish.

Events on that night, or at least the bringing-Buffy-back-from-the-dead part, got a little fuzzy in Willow's memory after the death of the fawn. There'd been chanting, and a snake, and candles, of course, black ones—the universal color for warding off evil spirits, although fat lot of good they had done that night. Somewhere in the Great Cosmic Things That Were it had apparently been decided that "evil spirits" were not the same as demons—go figure—because all the black candles and the incantations and the herbs hadn't done a damned thing to keep away the horde of motorcycle-riding demons that had shown up once they'd gotten the word that the big bad Slayer in Sunnydale was nothing but a not-very-smart microchip-brained robot.

Things hadn't gone very well after that. The before part had been okay, at least as far as Willow could remember. They'd intentionally kept Dawn out of this one, and with their candles lit and held high, Willow had mixed the ingredients for her spell—including the fawn's blood that the others had been told was "black market stuff"—and drawn the requisite bloody patterns across her own face. She'd followed that with a symbol on the ground, also made of blood, and had felt herself start to sort of . . . melt away at the edges as something deeper and more primal took up temporary residence inside her.

Things had been different then. *She* had been different then, willing to give it all for her friendship. She'd felt the skin of her arms split, had endured the agony, and if she hadn't exactly welcomed it, she hadn't fought against it, either. She hadn't known it was coming, so she'd been helpless to warn the others. It was a test, that's all, and she'd known *something* was coming; the best she'd been able to do was let Tara know that much. Tara had stopped Xander from intervening, and it had been doubly hard not to do so when

Willow's skin had begun to writhe and a snake had forced its way from her throat. But somewhere in the Universe there was apparently the ultimate Murphy's Law, and the gang of motorcycle demons had nearly ruined everything by crashing the end of the spell and shattering the Urn of Osiris. To this day, Willow believed that the abrupt ending of the spell was what had ended things so badly, bringing Buffy back to life when they didn't even know the spell had worked and leaving the Slayer buried alive.

But there would be none of that nonsense now.

Osiris had made it clear that Tara would not be resurrected like Buffy had been, that the method of Tara's death—supposedly a "natural" death as opposed to a supernatural one like Buffy's—forbade it. Osiris was certainly entitled to his opinion, but he wasn't the only God-fish in the big black of the Universal Ocean. It had taken a bit of research, but Willow had found another entity who had the power to do what she wanted. It might take some doing, but she was willing to try.

After all, she had only to convince the god to do her will.

Could she do it?

Of course. She *had* to.

But . . .

There it was, that secret seed of doubt in her heart that could ruin everything. She had to believe in herself, in her powers and her abilities. She *had* to—anything less was a weakness, and she would fail. And that was unthinkable.

And yet, how could she *help* doubting? Everything in the world seemed to be against her, everyone seemed to want to stand in her way despite the fact that she wasn't doing anything to warrant it. Even the Ghost of Tara, the spirit of her own precious love, insisted Willow was headed for failure. The only reason Willow couldn't let that prediction of doom influence her was because the Ghost of Tara had admitted that she couldn't always see the future, and she *had* occasionally been wrong, such as when she'd thought that putting Flo into a comatose state would ease her mind and instead it had subjected the young woman to endless nightmares. The very last thing that Willow could cling to was that if the Ghost of Tara could be wrong about other things, she could be wrong about this, too.

She had to be.

Chapter Eighteen

The graveyard was practically vibrating with power.

Willow could feel it in herself, of course, and also in the other women. The sensation was more than just a tingling in her bones and flesh and blood. It was almost like walking through a sort of cosmic soup— the energy was enough to make you have to *push* a little through the air as you moved from place to place. Had it been an electrical charge, she wouldn't have been surprised to see the ends of her own hair flaring straight up like the Bride of Frankenstein.

This was it—the most special night, the pinnacle of everything she had worked and fought for these past many weeks, the goal for which she had been willing to sacrifice everything. Every single thing tonight had to be just perfect: from the very clothes they wore, to the words and potions that would force Yama to come forth and face her. There would be no repeat of the nearly disastrous end that had happened when she'd brought Buffy back from the dead—she had a protection spell all lined up that would keep out anyone not involved in the spell. Yes, she was ready, and she hoped the rest of the coven was too. They weren't going to get another chance, and if they failed her tonight . . . well, no one wanted to go there.

Willow had put aside her normal clothes for tonight's ritual, and the rest of the women had done the same. They had dressed as she had requested, in robes of a dozen different colors representing everything from the sun to the earth to her own shimmering scarlet cloak, the color of life's blood and love. They'd brought dozens of candles to light the night and the altar to Yama that Willow carefully put together in front of Tara's grave.

The Ghost of Tara stood next to her, thankfully silent—of all times, tonight Willow didn't think she could stand to hear any more of the spirit's doubts. It was a beautiful sight, with the coven members adorned in their best for the ritual, the candlelight splitting the darkness all around like winking spots of starlight. Even adorned in her eternally bloody blouse, the Ghost of Tara herself shone like a spotlight amidst it all, and Willow had to believe that this was because she knew what was coming: the rejuvenation of her earthly body and the reuniting of her spirit within it.

The altar was carefully set out on a red velvet cloth at the head of Tara's grave, facing her headstone. The evidence of Willow's earlier visits was already there, and she removed it now, placing the stones to the side to make room. Before Willow opened the small mahogany chest that contained the summoning ingredients, she walked a solitary, wide circle around the grave and the coven members. In one hand she carried a lit white candle, in the other a red one—both strong symbols of protection. Their tiny flames left a trail of glittering smoke behind Willow as she muttered her simple but powerful protection spell along the way: *"Let no man or beast or creature cross this threshold until the morn, protect us within until we are done. Let no man or beast or creature . . ."* Around and around, three times, until Willow could feel in the trembling of her fingertips that the spell had taken and they were safe from intruders. Tonight there would be no repeat of the past—when she and the others looked overhead, the fruits of her protection incantation were visible all around them, as though the gods themselves had laced a shimmering bowl over the entire area.

It had taken some time to decide, but Willow had finally opted to arrange the coven members by age rather than by power, as a tribute to the seasons of life: childhood, youth, womanhood, maturity. She found it interesting that she was the youngest—born after Amy by only two months—but the most powerful. Past that, age seemed to have no relation to power level or knowledge, so clearly that was something that destiny had placed in the hands of each individual Wiccan; as was always the case, the outcome depended upon the person and what they did with their own life. Willow had made it clear that she wanted a celebration of the coming life, and color to welcome it, so they made a beautiful and colorful group in robes ranging from Willow's own crimson to Sying's sun-colored to Flo's midnight blue, like a rainbow awaiting the return of Tara's physical body.

So much research, so much effort into building up her power, and finally, Willow was ready. The others stood around her and held their candles up high, and as Willow carefully opened the chest, they began their slow, soft chant—

"We summon thee, Yama, Son of Surya and God of Death, on behalf of Willow, Wiccan and one left behind, who seeks the return of her beloved life mate, Tara. We summon thee, Yama, Son of Surya and God of Death . . ."

Their voices drowned out everything—the wind, the night birds, the rustling of the tree branches overhead. As the Wiccans kept up their quiet, singsong words, over and over, Willow dug her fingers deep into the mixture of summoning and protection herbs ground into a fine powder inside the chest. Filling her right palm with the fragrant substance, she brought it out and let it trail around in a slow, precise circle separating her from the other coven members. There were so many things blended together, but Willow felt attuned to each and every one of them: lotus, dandelion, sweetgrass, mullein, African violet, bayberry, papaya, spearmint, mulberry, calendula, clover, lime, comfrey, mimosa, frankincense, sage, mistletoe, thistle, pennyroyal, plum, anise, Saint John's-wort, and finally—appropriately—weeping willow. So many ingredients—surely that would be enough power to bring Yama, enough protection from his offensives, enough strength to defeat him. History was full of the evidence that gods had been defeated before. They could be again.

Willow *felt* Yama coming before he actually appeared, sensed him being pulled from whatever realm he rested in by the irresistible force of the coven's chant, her spell, and the sheer power of their force of will, of her *want*. As befitted a god, he came from everywhere and nowhere all at once—Willow was never quite sure. He seemed to surround her and the Ghost of Tara, and, of course, Tara's grave, with the only thing that contained him being that simple and so very fragile line of crushed herbs.

Everything in the Universe but her and Yama and Tara just . . . faded out of importance. The coven, the protective field around them, the stars in the heavens suddenly seemed so far away. For a long, breathless moment, Willow wasn't even sure there was air left— perhaps it was all for nothing, and she would die here tonight, her quest to resurrect Tara nothing but the stepping-stone to her own final journey that would ulti- mately, in its own way, finally reunite the two of them.

But no . . .

Destiny, it seems, preferred not to let her off so easy.

Yama towered over her. Willow had seen some incredible things in her life, and all of it in the rela- tively short period of time since Buffy Summers had come to live in Sunnydale and revealed the existence of the Hellmouth. Even so, all the research in the world hadn't prepared Willow Rosenberg for this—even the crazed she-god that Buffy had battled, Glory, had *nothing* on the ancient figure that glowered down at her now.

"What puny mortal *dares* to call upon me?" the god demanded. His withering gaze took in all the members of the coven and finally settled on Willow, but only after resting for a long, unsettling moment on the Ghost of Tara. Of all the things that had happened so far, that single look at the spirit made her heart stutter the most in fear. Why in God's name had it never occurred to her that she'd just brought into this world, right in front of her beloved, one of the very deities that could take Tara away from her forever?

"I did," Willow said, and stepped forward, placing herself between Yama and the Ghost of Tara. "My name is Willow." She sounded a whole lot bolder than she felt, especially given the sudden rush of unpleasant Glory-related memories that came crashing through her mind. But that was then, and Willow was now— and a whole lot more powerful. Glory's adversary had been Buffy, and let's face it: Today's Wicked Willow packed a lot more punch than one regular slayer any day.

"Insolent woman!" Yama hissed. He was huge, tall and wide enough to blot out the sky and the stars and the moon above them—had it not been for the candle-light held in the shaking hands of the other coven members, there would have been no light at all by which Willow could see. He had a monstrous, round belly crisscrossed with decorative beads from his blood-colored costume, and it was nothing like the friendly, roly-poly belly shown on a million Buddha statues around the world—it just made him look big and . . . *hungry.* Muscular arms wrapped in bands of carved copper protruded from wide, gleaming shoulders, and the hands at the end of each were thick-fingered and tipped by long, cruel fingernails. In one hand was a long staff made of some kind of dark, shining wood; in the other was something else she couldn't quite glimpse . . . a sword? Yes, it was definitely a long, carved sword. Willow didn't remember anything in her research that said he carried a bladed weapon, but that didn't mean it couldn't happen. In fact, with a god, *anything* could happen.

And just to drive that fact home, there was the matter of Yama's face.

In her research—extensive—on Hindu mythology, Willow had seen plenty of pictures and statues of this particular god, most of which had shown a somewhat benevolent-looking male figure, usually with an elaborate pointed headdress of the kind that was very common in the depiction of Hindu religion entities. Not as common were the ones that depicted the god she now faced: a snarling, heavy-faced creature that was more demon than man, and the farthest cry imaginable from the soothing purveyor of souls that a dead person would want to convey them into the afterlife. His lips were thick and drawn tight over large, pointed teeth, while a long, curving tongue swiped at the air, leaving droplets of spittle lingering in front of his chin. Horns sprouted from each side of his head, pushing upward from the midst of a swirl of heavy hair that gleamed like oiled ropes in the candlelight. A smell, unpleasant and animalistic, filled the air so heavily, it nearly made Willow choke, and she realized it was the stench of the water buffalo on which Yama rode. The beast stomped and snorted, layering the area in front of its head with the moist steam spewing from its flaring nostrils.

As if he was dismissing her, Yama suddenly widened his pit-black gaze until it once again settled on the Ghost of Tara. "You!" he exclaimed. His voice was heavy enough to make the ground shudder. "You have overstepped your bounds to be at the side of this mortal woman. You belong with me!" Yama leveled his wooden staff and pointed it toward Tara's spirit. "Come!"

"No!" In a startling move, Willow slapped aside the wooden pole. She vaguely heard the Ghost of Tara gasp behind her, but she couldn't be concerned with that—right now, she had to keep Yama firmly within her sights and away from Tara, to try to read his shocked expression and gauge how quickly that surprise was going to turn into fury. "In the manner of Savitri the Indian Princess, I challenge you for the right to win back the spirit of Tara Maclay and reunite it with her physical body!"

Yama's eyes widened as he pulled his dark gaze from Tara and stared down at Willow instead, more taken aback by her mettle in summoning him to begin with. For a moment the deep-set orbs glowed red. Then he laughed, and there was nothing at all pleasant about the sound.

"Another foolish human who believes in an old, impossible legend," he boomed. "I begin to believe that you mortals will never learn the difference between fact and fantasy."

"The two are sometimes separated by lines only the width of a spider's web," Willow shot back. "Of all things, you should realize the truth of that—your presence here tonight proves it!"

Yama leered at her, and beneath his immense weight, the water buffalo snorted and jerked. "The compassionate, generous god you seek is no more, mortal woman. Can you not tell that the eons that have transformed the world and made it a harder place have done the same to me?" The god tossed his head. "The ancient princess you speak of won the return of the spirit of her husband, Satyavan, through cleverness and unrelenting love." Suddenly Yama's head swung down low, impossibly so on what appeared to have been such a short neck, and his hideous face swayed back and forth in front of Willow's, only a few inches away from her nose. "Do you really think you can be as clever, little witch?"

Willow kept her shoulders straight and forced herself not to flinch. "Yes."

The god laughed again, the sound bubbling darkly in his wide, thick-skinned chest. "So foolish," he repeated. He twisted his head around and surveyed the other women, his eyes glittering. "There is not a one of you here tonight who is close to being Savitri's equal," he said when he finally faced Willow once more. "Savitri was the long-awaited daughter of a king, named after a goddess of the sun who granted the man a daughter when he had worshipped and prayed and sacrificed for eighteen years! She had eyes like the sun goddess who willed her into existence, and such was her radiance that she was often mistaken for a goddess herself. So beautiful and strong and wise was Savitri that, despite her desires, no man would ask for her hand in marriage, and finally she was forced to seek out on her own a man she would have as her husband. But the one she found and loved, the man to whom she pledged herself forever, was destined to die within a year."

"I know all this," Willow said. "I—"

"You know *nothing*!" Yama bellowed at her. His arms flailed angrily, and despite her resolve, Willow couldn't suppress a startled inhalation. She barely stopped herself from making a disastrous back-step into the protective line of powder.

For a moment, Yama towered over her, breathing hard, then the god seemed to collect himself so he could continue. "Savitri was unable to stop me from pulling Satyavan's spirit from his body, but in her quest to see it restored, she thought not of herself first, but of her family, and of Satyavan's family. Only after *they* had been well-provided for did she turn to the request that made it impossible for me not to replace her husband's spirit in his body—that of being the mother to many of his children." Yama glowered at Willow. "It was then, and only then, that I replaced the likeness of himself within Satyavan's breast and returned him to life."

Willow swallowed. "Then you can do the same for Tara."

Yama grinned at her, showing his long, pointed teeth. "And why should I? Who are *you,* Willow Rosenberg? What have you *done* to show to me that bests or is equal to the virtue of the long-dead Princess Savitri?"

Willow lifted her chin. "I have love," she said simply. "For Tara. The kind that never ends, even when faced with the barrier of death. The kind for which—"

"You would kill," Yama finished for her. His frightening grin twisted into an unpleasant grimace. "Your ignorance truly amazes me, witch. How do you compare the offerings of a pure spirit with one such as yourself? You have nothing to offer me but shame."

Willow was stunned. Her mouth worked, but she was so angry, she literally couldn't speak—her lungs hitched, all the muscles in her face moved, but nothing, *nothing,* would come out. "Shame?" she finally croaked.

Yama spread his arms wide, and his water buffalo snorted again, showering Willow and the others with its hot breath. "You know your own failures, the same ones that all manifested after the death of your lover. Must I list them here for everyone to witness?" Before she could respond, he did so anyway, swiping the air each time with the wickedly hungry edge of his sword as though he were carving the words into the very fabric of the world. "You have violated the most sacred of laws, Willow Rosenberg. You have *murdered*—"

"But the man killed Tara!" Willow cried. Her

fists were balled uselessly at her side. "Warren murdered *her*!"

"IT WAS NEVER MEANT THAT YOU SHOULD BE HIS EXECUTIONER!" Yama bellowed.

The god's breath, a hundred times more meaty and rancid than the water buffalo's, rolled over her and nearly made Willow gag. Even so, she couldn't stop the scream that welled out of her insides and went right back at the deity. *"I don't care—he DESERVED what he got!"*

Yama drew himself up and folded his arms, the staff and sword sliding neatly out of sight. "And that," he said in a much softer and more ominous tone, "is exactly the point. You don't *care.*"

Willow frowned and scrubbed at her face. "What? I don't . . . I don't understand. Of course I care. I . . ." Her voice faded as she realized how contradictory she sounded, but how else was she going to be able to explain herself?

Yama jerked his head at the Ghost of Tara and the other coven members, all standing so still, they might have been just more examples of the stone statuary scattered around the old cemetery. "But only for yourself."

Willow shook her head vehemently. "No—you're wrong. I care for Tara."

Yama's dark laughter boiled around her. "Please, witch—do you think me blind? Your revenge has taken the life of one man when it was not your right to take *anyone's* life. Had his two accomplices not escaped, you would have tripled the black marks against your soul without so much as a second thought." Yama's hellish eyes heated up again, burning into her as they brightened to deep scarlet. "Your greed regarding your dead lover has not only ripped her spirit from the netherworld, but wrongly bound it to your side."

Willow's mouth went dry. Ripped from the netherworld? Had she done the same thing to Tara that she'd unknowingly done to Buffy? No, of course not—Yama was wrong. She hadn't had anything to do with the Ghost of Tara's return. Tara's spirit had done that all on her own, and it had been a complete surprise to Willow when she'd first appeared. Yama was deceiving her, entertaining himself by playing a cruel and macabre game with her conscience and her mind. She would not fall for this; she would not allow him to toy with her. "I want her back," she said rigidly.

Yama nodded sagely. "I'm sure you do. But what about the others—Anan and Njeri—whom you've sacrificed in your demand for Tara's return? Perhaps they have loved ones who would also like *them* back. . . . In fact, Anan *did* have such a person." Yama glanced at Flo, then his lips stretched back until they nearly formed a snarl. "And where is *she* this night? Why, right *there,* forced to stand in servitude because you care nothing for her pain, or for *her.* For you, there is only yourself and your own emptiness, and you would sacrifice anything to see it filled!"

"As did Savitri," Willow said stubbornly. "She faced you and was granted the return of her husband's spirit! Why can I not do the same?"

Suddenly the god's claw-tipped hands were folded

around her shoulders, gripping and burning and feeling like they would sink deep into her flesh. This close up, his breath wasn't just foul—it was *hot,* scorching the surface of her skin as though she'd stayed too long under a salon tanning lamp. "Because you are *dirty,*" he told her, and the words reverberated though her bones and her skin and her teeth, through everything that she was now. "Princess Savitri would have sacrificed herself but no one else. You would sacrifice everyone *but* yourself."

He drew back and stared down at her, and Willow could see her own reflection in the black pools of his gaze. Her figure looked small and insignificant, a woman of absolutely no consequence in the presence of this strong-willed god of death.

But . . . *impure?*

How dare he say such a thing. There was no greater affection, no *purer* love, than that nourished by one who would sacrifice everything for the life of the other.

Obviously the application for being a god didn't require a Cupid's degree.

Yama drew himself up, then lifted a heavy, gilt-edged leather rein from the neck of the water buffalo. He shook it a couple of times, then pulled back on it until the great beast raised its head and snorted angrily. His gaze racked the area again, then settled inexorably on the Ghost of Tara.

Yama had ignored her request. He was leaving.

And he intended to take the Ghost of Tara with him.

"NO!" Willow screeched. Before she could think

or plan or contemplate what she was about to do, her hands were charged and full of fire and energy, and the hair on her arms and head was nearly standing straight up with fury. She sent all the anger manifesting in her palms straight toward the head of this otherwordly being who was going to steal the very last visage of the woman she loved.

Willow's twin fireballs caught Yama completely by surprise—clearly he'd never expected a mere mortal woman, even a witch, to disregard his word and try to fight him. The blast struck him square between the eyes and rocked him backward on his water buffalo, and the creature's snort of surprise bled immediately into a bellow of pain as sparks and bits of burning fabric and hair spiraled down onto its back. It bucked a couple of times and tried to rear up, but Yama wasn't going to be unseated—the deity was probably melded with the beast and its saddle, almost like a centaur. A yank on the reins and the water buffalo crashed back to the ground, its front hooves pawing angrily at the dirt.

"You give me back my Tara!" Willow screamed at the deity. Before he could react, she threw another round at him, this time everything she could pull together. Her skin crackled and smoked, and the energy hammering out of her fingertips looked like liquid lightning; it struck Yama and his beast of burden and spread over them like an blanket of blue-and-white electricity, spiderwebbing their entire forms. The water buffalo howled and staggered sideways as Yama's muscular back arched and he threw his head back in agony.

"I'll *destroy* you," Willow spat at him. She inhaled and *pulled,* gathering power from herself and the others for a third strike, then—

Yama's broadsword whistled through the air in front of her.

Her breath left her lungs in an involuntary rush, like someone had let all the air out of her balloon. For a long moment she didn't understand what had happened; then she looked down and saw a line of blood, thin and painful but not deadly, blossom across a horizontal split in the front of her robe at waist level.

She ground her teeth and hit him again without looking up, knowing he would expect her to see her target, not aim blind.

Willow's reward was hearing his second scream of agony, loud enough to make her head ache and definitely worthy of a god. The water buffalo's wailing only added to the sound of her impending success—she cared nothing at all for the mystical creature, and if it died because she'd defeated its owner, then so be it. Before she would attack him again, Willow passed a quick hand over her abdomen to heal it and—

Nothing happened.

She blinked. There was no healing of the stinging sensation across her belly, no knitting of her flesh. Fresh blood still stained her crimson robe, making the fabric darker around the long slash in it. Something was wrong. How could she not be able to heal herself?

For a moment—one that was just a wolf's breath too long—she was caught off guard.

And Yama retaliated.

If she'd imagined that the power she'd hit him with—something vaguely reminiscent of supercharged electrical energy—was painful, it was *nothing* like what he did to her. One second she was looking at her wound in confusion, the next she was struggling to pull nothing at all into her lungs—her air was *gone,* or maybe it had been replaced by something much too huge to fit into her windpipe and be processed by her lungs, because she couldn't breathe, she couldn't *breathe,* she couldn't *BREATHE.* Willow's feet left the ground as she was pulled upward, but she didn't feel that either—she was much too busy trying to find air somewhere, *anywhere.* Her hands curled into claws and spasmed—

Then she fell out of the air and landed in a heap on the graveyard soil.

But she wasn't through fighting, oh not by a long shot. Snarling, Willow was back on her feet instantly, yanking power from herself and all the other women, and flinging it at Yama even as he stood back and started to gloat down at her. Then they were trading mystical blows back and forth and back and forth, and with each lift and twitch of Yama's cruel, omnipotent hands, Willow's strength faded more and her body bore a continually growing set of painful, bloody wounds.

God help her—and Tara—but she was going to lose.

"No!" she cried. *"Nooooo!"* Her face was streaked with tears as she jerked around to face the members of her coven. But she would find no help there—they were completely done in. Foolish her, she'd had no concept of the power necessary to fight this being, and all the women—even the so-powerful Amy—were drained and trembling, barely able to stand and hold the candle line. She'd used them up as surely as a vampire sucked its victim of every last ounce of life blood.

Fire crisscrossed her stomach, and Willow gasped as the edge of Yama's sword sang through the air in front of her again—he was teasing her, cutting her to ribbons, but no more, just for the fun of it. Her legs bucked, and she went to her knees in front of Yama, wondering why he didn't just kill her and be done with it. She was hollow now, with nothing left inside to fight him with. Why—

"How does it feel, Willow Rosenberg?" Yama's baritone voice boomed in her ears, healthy and strong, not a bit worse for the wear caused by her repeated and apparently useless magickal blows. "You think you can defeat me—a god—because you have enough power to play the parasite on those around you." Yama laughed, and the sound was loud and obnoxious enough to make her nauseated. She couldn't stop herself from leaning over and retching above the ground. She tasted liquid, thick and metallic, then spat out a mouthful of blood. Its scarlet hue matched the growing stain across her stomach.

"Feel it," Yama commanded. The cheerful, playful tone of his voice changed to something darker and demanding. Fear coursed through Willow despite her despair and the fact that she'd already resigned herself to her upcoming death. Without Tara, she had no reason to live anyway.

"It burns, doesn't it?" Yama glared down at her. He

looked strong and capable, eyes clear and burning red again, carrying himself as though nothing had even happened—all that power that Willow had hoarded, all the weeks and weeks of collecting it, and he hadn't even been *fazed*. People had *died* in Willow's pursuit of enough power to triumph over this deity. How shameful was it that they had done so for nothing?

"Think of the people you have hurt in your quest to do this, you foolish witch," Yama boomed at her. "Consider the pain you feel now, and compare it to the agony felt by the three you would have fed alive to creatures from the netherworld—two men and a young woman who once trusted you with their lives and who would have done anything to help you, had you only *asked*."

Willow wanted to stand and fight, but no matter how she willed her body to move, it would not respond—she was simply too tired, too beaten down in the ever-ongoing quest to resurrect Tara. Her coven was nearly at its end, and she could see the women out of the corner of her eye, themselves fighting to stay on their feet, struggling, still, to support her and do her will. And really . . . *why*? What had she done for them in return? What had she done to *deserve* the power and the effort they'd expended on her behalf? For the first time since Tara's death, Willow could see herself through their eyes, her greed and her demands, her single-minded goal that would destroy anyone and everything that stood in her way, even her oldest and once dearest friends.

Yama's mouth twisted in disgust as he stared down

at her. "You are a blight upon everything that love stands for, Willow Rosenberg. The honorable Princess Savitri thought only of others in her campaign to save her beloved Satyavan, while you think only of yourself. Even Tara, whom you claim to cherish so much and whose spirit and misery is imprisoned between this world and the next because of your rapacity, has escaped your notice."

"Please," Willow whispered. "Don't take her from me. I can't—"

Yama's heavy eyebrows raised, and he gestured at the women surrounding them. "'Please'? Now there is a word that your consorts are hearing for the very *first time* since you pressed them to serve you! How quickly you forgot the cardinal rule of your Wiccan kind: Nothing you do shall be for personal gain." Yama shook his head, and his hair swirled wildly in the air. "It is a testimony to my own generosity and your own undeserved *luck,* Willow Rosenberg, that I even let you *live* this night." He reached down with the hand gripping the sword and slid the blade beneath her chin, then forced her head up so that she had nowhere else to look but at his burning gaze. "You will bind Tara Maclay to this world no longer. She will cross over without you, and what you do from this day forth is not my concern. Perhaps one day you will lose your blindness and see the world around you as you once did, and you will know that it was not Tara who made you see it that way, but *yourself* who made it that way for Tara."

Yama drew his sword away, leaving another stinging line of pain under her chin. "My wounds on your body will heal, and the scars will eventually fade. It is up to you to decide what you have learned."

Before Willow could think of a way to respond, could come up with some kind of plea to make the deity change his mind, Yama sheathed his sword in one motion, then snatched up the Ghost of Tara. The spirit didn't even look surprised, as if she had known all along that this would be her ultimate fate. Of course she had—hadn't she warned Willow over and over that the resurrection would not succeed? Hadn't Willow's own stubbornness made her refuse to accept the Ghost of Tara's wisdom?

The Ghost of Tara suddenly blazed within Yama's grip, but the expression on her translucent face was anything but fear or pain—it was rapturous, as if what was happening to her was something she'd waited eons for. Straining to see upward, Willow felt even more guilt load itself onto what she was already carrying. Yama had been right: She had tied the Ghost of Tara here out of her own desperate need, steadfastly ignoring her dead lover's pleas for freedom in favor of her own selfishness. While Tara had been starving for eternity, Willow had hungered for the fleeting here and now.

There was a flash, and everything that was Tara's spirit abruptly disintegrated into a frantically sparkling circle of light floating above Yama's dark-skinned palm. Yama gave Willow a final, withering glance, then his body and that of the huge water buffalo's began to fold in on itself, over and over, getting smaller each time. Five times, six, seven—

And Yama disappeared, taking all that remained of the Ghost of Tara with him.

Chapter Nineteen

"**I**'m going over to Willow's," Buffy announced, as if it were the most natural thing in the world.

"What?" Giles said. As Buffy slipped on her jacket, his mouth worked as if she'd walked by and popped something nasty into it. "You're going—wait!"

"Oh, that is so at the top of the 'this is not a good idea' list," Dawn said. They'd forgone the dubious comfort of the Magic Box for Buffy's house, and she'd been sitting on the overstuffed couch with her feet propped up on the coffee table; she still tired easily since the ordeal in the cave, and the nightmares she had each night weren't helping matters any. "In fact, why don't we file it away under 'things to do never.'"

"Second that," Xander put in. "And third it too."

"Dawn's right," Giles said quickly. "There really isn't any reason to—"

"Wrong," Buffy cut in. "There's *plenty* of reason. We can't just sit back and ignore the fact that she's out there, and that she's changed into the kind of person who would do what she did to you guys." Her gaze touched each of them. "This isn't the Willow we knew, guys. She's a *killer,* and she needs to be stopped."

"Actually, if you leave her alone, I think she'll forget about us," Anya said. "'Live and let live' and all that. Those might be words to live by . . . literally."

"'Killer' is kind of a harsh word, don't you think?" Xander scratched his head. "'Vigilante' sounds better."

"But not true," Dawn told him. "Buffy's a vigilante."

"I am not!"

"Sure you are," Dawn insisted. "I bet if you look up 'Slayer' in the mystical dictionary, you'll find 'vigilante.' Willow's just out for revenge."

Buffy frowned at her sister. "I still don't think 'vigilante' fits what I do. That's like a bunch of people running around unsupervised with rope and looking for a big tree."

"Buffy's right," Giles began. "She—"

"First *I* was right, now it's Buffy." Dawn folded her arms. "Make up your mind."

"Well, it's two different topics. You can't expect to—"

"Can we get back on the Willow track here?" Buffy asked. "I'm totally sympathetic about how she wants to bring Tara back, but she just can't go around flaying people alive and burning them up, then feeding *us* to demons to get it done. That's not right."

"Hard to argue with Sister Logic," Dawn muttered.

"But let's not forget that Your Slayerness hasn't been enough to de-Willowfy Sunnydale," Anya pointed out. She glanced around the living room. "The new rustic look of the Magic Box is great—not—but do you really want to chance bringing that here?"

Dawn answered before Buffy could. "I'm going to make an executive decision and say no." She gave her older sister a hard look. "Rah rah rah to the cause of good, but I think we've offered up enough flesh this time around."

Buffy was silent for a few seconds. "Guys, I can't just let this go," she finally said. She spread her hands. "Yeah, she healed you, and you're almost as good as new, but don't forget that she did the dirty deed to begin with. What kind of person would do that to people she knew loved her? What kind of person is she *now*?" She shook her head, then sighed. "I'll tell you what—I'll just try to talk to her, see what's going on, what's coming up."

"I think it's a mistake," Giles said stiffly. "I think it's dangerous and foolish."

Buffy scowled at him. "I get that," she said. "But I also can't just roll over and play dead and hope that she doesn't notice us when she decides to take her next diabolical leap. It's not what we do—it's not what *I* do."

No one said anything for a long moment, then Xander cleared his throat. "I'll go with you," he said.

"No way," Buffy said immediately. "That's way too dangerous."

"I'm going," he said stubbornly. Without waiting

for a response, he pulled his own jacket off the hallway chair and shrugged it on. "I've known Willow longer than anyone here. Maybe I can . . . I don't know, talk to her or something—*reach* her."

"Take him with you," Giles said. "We all know that Willow is quite angry with you, and that she doesn't see that the circumstances surrounding Tara's death were beyond your control. Perhaps Xander's right—out of all of us, he has the least ties to anything supernatural on which she can place blame. She might listen to him. It's worth a chance, anyway."

"You'll pardon me for sitting this one out with Giles," Anya said. "I'm really quite tired of Willow throwing me bodily through the air. In fact, I'm feeling even less diplomatic than usual about the whole thing."

Xander raised one eyebrow in Anya's direction. "Diplomatic? You? By any chance did you check the dictionary for the definition—"

"Well, I'm definitely in," Dawn said firmly. She stood, and even did a good job of not looking scared or shaky. "It's a backup thing—the more the merrier."

Buffy started to automatically shake her head, then relented. Why not? She wasn't duping anyone. Anya was right, and it was very likely she was going to get her posterior thoroughly kicked yet again. At least Xander and Dawn would be there to drag the pieces back home. "All right."

Provided, of course, that Willow didn't turn on them, too.

Again.

• • •

It was almost dawn when Willow finally got back to her building.

If there was anything more indicative of what had happened, this squat and ugly concrete building said it all—even though it was still dark, gone was the mystically shimmering sea-colored surface that had beautified its exterior and camouflaged the doors and windows. She hadn't even realized the hidden effort it had taken to maintain appearances, but with such a big chunk of her energy expended, here was undeniable proof. It was like a mondo-size TSR—a terminate and stay resident computer program—that had suddenly lost its cloaking properties and overrun the operating system with some kind of huge, unsightly icon on the computer screen.

There hadn't been much to say to the others back at the cemetery. To be honest, the idea of failing—really *failing*—had never been in her mental repertoire, and she'd had no Plan B on which she could fall back. No one—not even Amy—had tried to comfort her, and it was just as well; it didn't take much to imagine her lashing out at the first person to come within range. The women had drifted away one by one, snuffing out their candles when they were sure that Willow was defeated and there was nothing left inside her—or them—to call the god back and try again. And after a while, a very *short* while, Willow had found herself in the cemetery and truly alone.

She'd replaced the visitor stones on Tara's grave, then sat there for a long time, staring at her beloved's headstone, reading and rereading the words, trying to accept the fact that she'd fought and she'd *lost,* not just her battle with Yama, but the Ghost of Tara, her last fragile link to the woman she loved.

Now Willow stared up at the warehouse, seeing but not really seeing the stained concrete, the tin sides with the long, bloody-looking rust stains. All the pretty to it was gone, all the fancy hide-everything costume. It was very much like her life—all this time she'd been hiding behind the belief that she could resurrect Tara when everything had pointed to a truth she'd refused to accept: In this, of all things, she would never, *ever* succeed, no matter how much power she managed to gather.

She had never experienced such crushing disappointment in her life.

With sudden, gut-wrenching clarity, Willow realized that for far too long she had intentionally pushed aside the cruelest fact: Since that fateful day, her dead lover had been nothing but a ghost, and the memories that had carried her through Tara's most recent absence and imprisonment at the Magic Box had been of a *living* Tara, not a dead one. She had been doomed to fail right from the start and she had ignored it, and even had she failed and been left with the Ghost of Tara rather than her physical body, what would have happened then? More disappointment—her life, and the Ghost of Tara's sad, tormented spiritual existence, would have only been a pale shadow of what she and Tara once were.

So what was left? Nothing, that's what. No joy, no love. There was only pain, and it wasn't just hers. Oh, no—the world was *full* of it, like some kind of big, hollow ball stuffed with agony. Proportionately speaking, the pain-to-joy ratio was so far off, she couldn't imagine why anyone even bothered anymore. After all, what did they have to gain? Some fleeting moment of happiness, and then what? Sickness, illness, murder, death. It all ended in death eventually anyway. Decades of struggling to work and make a living, love and be loved, and what happened? A visit from Osiris, or from Yama, or from God, or from whatever particular deity decided to pick a person's personal number from that big old universal pot.

So, really . . . why bother?

"Willow."

She whirled, and wouldn't you know it, there were three of her old buds: Buffy, Xander, and Dawn. It was just as she'd been thinking: You struggled and you fought and you got pain, and then what happened? You were stupid and you came back, and you got some more. "Now is a really bad time for a reunion," she told them in a hoarse voice.

But Buffy only stared at her, conflicting emotions running across her face. "Willow, what happened to you? You look . . . well, awful!"

Willow grimaced. She *felt* awful, so of course she probably looked the part. Tonight she'd been beaten and squeezed and suffocated, and she'd had everything she'd worked for destroyed. She wasn't going to hold her breath for a winning spot in the current round of life's beauty pageant. "Thanks for your concern," she snapped. "Now would you just leave me alone?"

"Not this time," Buffy said firmly. "We need to

talk. To"—she hesitated, not really sure what to say—
"to resolve things once and for all."

Willow laughed, and the sound bubbled out of her
throat like broken glass rumbling from her lungs.
"Once and for all? Oh, yeah—you have no idea."

When Buffy would have stepped forward, Xander
frowned at Willow and placed his hand on Buffy's arm
to stop her. "Willow . . . what's happened to you?"

Willow rolled her eyes. "Oh, please—don't tell me
you've done the short-term-memory-loss thing already.
Do I really have to go back to that whole Warren-
killed-Tara thing and explain it all over again?"

Xander shook his head. "No, I don't mean that. I
mean *now,* since we last saw you—something else has
gone wrong, something horrible. I can tell."

Willow stared at him, then something about her . . .
sagged. It was an almost imperceptible movement, but
Xander had spent too much time with Willow not to
catch it. This was bad, *really* bad, and her next words
confirmed his fears. She was looking right at him, but
he could have sworn she was seeing something else,
something bigger and more profound that existed in
the air around him, and which he would never understand. She gave a brittle, small-sounding laugh and
tried to shrug. "It was all for . . . nothing, you know?
Gathering the power, creating the demons, fighting
with them." She blinked and focused again on Buffy.
"Fighting with *you.* I mean, people *died,* and not just
that worm Warren. I caused all that pain to try to end
my own, and you know what?" She raised her hands
and massaged her temples as though she had a massive

headache. Her fingernails were as black as her eyes and lips. "All I did was make *more* pain. For other people, for myself. In the end, that's all there is—pain. For me, for you, for everyone in the world."

Dawn swallowed and took a tiny step forward. "It's not all like that, Willow. There's good stuff too. There's love, and friendship, and—"

Willow shook her head violently enough to make Dawn move back to where she'd started. "Oh, no. Not true—the truth is that everyone *thinks* there's always going to be more. That their next love or luck or great job or that ridiculous, elusive winning lottery ticket is always just around the corner or will happen tomorrow, or next week, or next month. But it won't happen, it'll *never* happen. Lovers leave—they die or they cheat or they just go away—and people get laid off and lose their houses and everything else, and they fight and fight and fight and it's all for nothing, because all anyone ever gets is absolutely *nowhere*."

Buffy stared at her, trying to comprehend not what Willow was saying, but what she was *feeling*. In spite of her fury at all the things Willow had done, she felt the sting of tears building behind her eyes. "Willow, it's not that bad—sure, we fight and we lose, but sometimes we win, too. In the end, it's worth it—"

Willow held up a hand, cutting off the rest of Buffy's sentence. "No, it's not." She tilted her head. "You know, it's been like this since I took all that power from Giles in the Magic Box, but I've been concentrating so hard on trying to bring back Tara that I pushed it to the back of my mind." She gave another of her sad, brittle laughs. "Of course, tonight I've been taught—*very* thoroughly—that I can't bring back Tara, so now there's nothing between me and all that emotion. All that *pain*."

Dawn's lower lip trembled. "You can't . . ."

"She's gone forever, isn't she?" Xander asked softly. "That's what this was all about. That's what happened tonight."

Willow raised her face toward the sky, as if she were trying to feel a breeze that wasn't there, an essence that was now forever out of her reach. "That's what it was *always* about. But I failed, and without that goal, there's nothing between me and the rest of the world. And all its agony."

"Willow, it doesn't have to be that way," Buffy said. "You can stop."

Willow's head swiveled toward Buffy jerkily, as though the bones in her neck were moving on old, rusty bearings. "Yeah, I can," she said suddenly. A sort of dark realization bloomed behind her eyes. "I have to. I'll stop it—I'll make it *all* go away."

Xander's eyes widened as he thought he suddenly understood the turn her thoughts had taken. "Oh, no. No, no, no—"

Willow inhaled, then her expression softened. "You poor bastards. Your suffering has to end too. But you live to fight, don't you? You always have."

"Willow, don't do this," Xander said urgently. He stepped toward her at the same time that Buffy did, but suddenly none of them could move—clearly, Willow had doused them with Wiccan glue.

"Don't do what?" Dawn asked. Her expression was laced with dread. "What'd I miss?"

"You won't miss a thing, Dawn," Willow said soothly. "The world's suffering will end, and yours will too, right along with it."

"Will, you can't murder the whole world!" Buffy exclaimed. "Come on, don't you think that's overreacting more than a little?"

"Really? Even when there's so little in the world that's actually good, so few people who actually treat one another with any decency?" She studied the three of them for a few moments, watching as they still struggled to move. "Call it 'murder' if you want to," Willow said blandly, "but I'd consider it a mercy killing. And you, Buffy—always wanting to fight, aren't you? You won't go out without a fight, and I really don't have time for one. But I guess it wouldn't be right for you to go out doing anything else. Enjoy your final battle, because in another half hour, you'll die along with everyone else."

And Willow clapped her hands and the lights abruptly went out for all three of them.

Chapter Twenty

"Anya, I'm afraid I have some bad news."

Anya jerked upright from where she'd been counting the number of freeze-dried eye-sucker lizards for the monthly inventory sheet. They were handy little things if you ground them to a powder and mixed them into love potions—they'd let the person doing the spell (usually a woman) see if her insignificant other was cheating on her, even if the two-timing jerk was doing it out of town. They were good sellers, so in the spirit of American enterprise, this month she'd raised the price by forty percent.

"Bad news?" She and Giles had decided to go to the Magic Box and get a little work done—there was certainly always enough of *that*—while they waited to hear about the outcome of Buffy's visit with Willow. Now Anya turned, vaguely aware that her fingers had curled around the edge of her clipboard so tightly that they hurt. "What bad news? Has something happened to Xander again? Or is Willow on her way here to destroy the Magic Box a second time?"

"Actually, something's going to happen to *all* of us," Giles said morosely. He held up a stone pottery bowl that Anya recognized as one of the new but extremely rare items in the shop. It was supposed to be Celtic, fashioned longer ago than Giles had the expertise to identify. "The history of this item claims that leaves dried from a tea made of sunflowers and spread in the bottom can accurately foretell spells of magickal importance."

Anya swallowed. "I can't believe I'm going to ask this, but I can't seem to stop myself. What do you mean by 'magickal importance'?"

Giles didn't seem to want to look at her, and she had to strain to hear him. "Spells such as those that are mean to . . ." He hesitated.

"Come on, Giles. I've always hated mysteries."

"Spells that are meant to destroy the world."

"Oh," was all she could finally manage.

He held the bowl out again, this time tilting it so she could see inside. The mass of dried leaves and the patterns they made meant nothing to her, of course, but what was interesting—and creepy—was that even though Giles tilted it to a nearly forty-five-degree angle, not a single piece of dried matter within the bowl shifted out of place against the nearly petrified pottery surface. Talk about having your future set in stone.

"Willow's going to destroy the world," Giles said softly.

Despite his soft tone, Anya thought her ears actually starting *ringing* at his words. "Well, we've got to stop her!" Her voice came out louder than she intended, nearly at shouting volume, and she had to fight to get herself and her panic level, which suddenly seemed to have become a separate entity all its own, under control. "Clearly we can't let her do that. I mean, we all live here!" She made a jerky motion in the air with one hand. "Do something—a spell or an incantation. *Something!*"

"Unfortunately, that won't stop her." Giles turned away and set the pottery bowl carefully on the counter. "Not based on what the tea leaves say she's doing." The former Watcher finally found enough courage to raise his haunted gaze to hers. "I'm sorry to say that the best I can offer you is the chance to find Xander and say your good-byes."

Buffy, Xander, and Dawn came back to consciousness facedown and with their mouths full of dirt.

"Oh, gross," Dawn said. "Where the heck are we, anyway?" She spat, then pushed herself upright and spat again. "I think that was a bug."

Xander scanned the dirt walls around them, then peered overhead. "I think we're in some kind of under- ground tomb. Oh, and bugs have a lot of protein," he added helpfully. He rolled onto his back, then grunted as he levered himself into a sitting position. "More than eighty percent of the plants on Earth are poisonous to man, but nearly all insects are edible."

"Could you be any *less* appetizing?" Buffy demanded. She was already on her feet, dusting angrily at her clothes. "How did she do that, anyway? I thought Anya said witches could only teleport themselves." She peered upward, but the ragged entrance to this not-so-homey hole in the ground they found themselves trapped in was a good fifteen feet above them, and there wasn't a handhold in sight. Great. Why did everything always seem to revolve around filthy holes in the ground?

"I think Willow has gone waaaaay beyond your average witch," Xander reminded her. "There's no telling *what* she can do nowadays."

"Oh, surprise me." Dawn pointed to the piles of debris and dirt surrounding them and the objects jutting at odd angles here and there. "What's this? Old bones, broken-up coffins, rotting clothes. Welcome to the latest of Sunnydale Cemetery hot spots." She grimaced. "At least I don't see any demons . . . yet."

"Xander?"

Xander scrambled to his feet and turned in a quick circle. "Anya? Where are you—"

"I'm up here."

The three of them craned their necks and they could just see Anya peeking over the edge of the hole.

"I can't get too close to the edge—it's crumbling. I'll fall over and end up a prisoner down there like you."

"Marvelous," Xander muttered. "I suppose it would be too much to hope for a ro—"

Something heavy whapped him on the side of the head.

"Ow!"

"I want you to come up and spend your final moments with me," Anya called down.

Xander, Buffy, and Dawn glanced at one another. "Final moments?" Xander craned his neck so he could see her. "I kind of thought we might be working things out."

"That doesn't matter anymore." She didn't say anything for a moment, and when he squinted upward, he saw her glancing nervously around. "Things just got a whole lot worse."

Buffy peered up at her. "How worse?"

Even from down here, they could see how distressed Anya looked. "End-of-the-world worse. Willow's going to destroy it. We don't have much time."

"Wait," Buffy said. "By 'it' . . . you mean destroy the world? She really *meant* it?"

"The world *world*?" Dawn asked. "As in whole and uncharted?"

"Yes," Anya confirmed. "Now come on, Xander. We don't have much time. We're just lucky that I could find you this time. The last time Willow kidnapped you, your whereabouts didn't show up when I scryed. I think it's because Gnarls are impervious to most magickal spells."

Xander turned to Buffy. "You go," he told her. "Get to Willow and—"

"Buffy can't do anything about it this time," Anya interrupted impatiently. "Giles said that no magick or supernatural force can stop her."

"What does *that* mean?" Buffy demanded. "I'm

not just going to sit here while Willow incinerates what I've been chosen to protect. I *have* to stop her!"

"I don't know!" Anya's voice was shrill with frustration. "He read in the tea leaves or something that 'the Slayer can't stop her.'"

They were all silent for a moment, then Dawn just had to ask: "So the big boom that she's cooking up is going to come down on us how?"

They could see Anya looking to her left and right, then she rattled the rope impatiently. "Giles said she's going to this big old Satanic temple on Kingman's Bluff."

Buffy frowned. "There's no temple on Kingman's Bluff."

Anya's head bobbed up and down. "There is—it's the Temple of Proserpexa."

Buffy's mouth worked. "Pro . . . serpexa? Who the hell is *that*?"

"A she-demon," Anya explained. "Way up there in the hierarchy. Her followers intended to use her effigy to destroy the world, but they all died when her temple got swallowed up in the earthquake of thirty-two."

Buffy stared upward. "So seventy years later, Willow's going to make their dreams come true."

Anya nodded, and her voice echoed down over them. She sounded calm and bright, all at the same time, like a news reporter talking about the evening's big disaster. "She's going to drain the planet's life force, funnel its energy through Proserpexa's effigy, and burn the earth to a cinder."

Buffy balled her fists. "And I can't do anything about this?"

"Nope. Not a thing."

Xander suddenly grabbed the rope and wrapped it around Dawn's waist paratrooper-style. "Get us out of here, Anya! I need to talk to Willow!"

"Oh, all right." Even from way down here, they could see Anya looked less than pleased. "But I don't think it's going to do any good and you're going to be wasting our last half hour alive talking to her when we could go somewhere and have until-death-do-us-part sex."

"I so did not need that image," Dawn said. "Especially considering it's going to be one of my last."

"No way," Xander said. "She'll—Buffy, *look out*!"

Buffy whirled and ducked automatically as something dark and grainy swung at her from the shadows. She retaliated automatically, and her fist met hard-packed dirt and bone; the teeth of a skeletal figure clacked hard together as her blow hammered it backward. "Oh, great," she said. "I guess Willow meant it when she said I should go down fighting." She jerked her finger toward Dawn. "Xander, get her out of here."

"Not," Dawn snapped. Before Buffy or Xander realized what she was doing, she'd yanked the rope away from her waist and was circling Xander with it. "You go, *now*. Willow might listen to you, but she doesn't give a bat's butt about me—she made that clear a bunch of times." Xander started to protest, and Dawn pushed him away, hard. "Save it. Buffy's going to need help down here." She jabbed a finger toward the darker recesses of the cave they were in. "Look down there."

Xander and Buffy obeyed automatically, and were

anything but heartened to see that the darkness was *moving,* filled with more darkness and the vibration of black shapes. Buffy's eyes narrowed. "You know," she said, "it's never a good idea to drop in on the dead."

"Xander, *go!*" Dawn commanded. "While you can still get out of here without some dead guy hanging on to your rear end!"

"Ditto that," Xander said, and jerked his face upward. "Anya—*pull!*"

She didn't need to be told again, and just to be sure, she morphed into vengeance-demon mode to gain extra strength. It didn't take a whole lot of effort on the part of her demon self to yank Xander up and out of the buried tomb, but when Xander cleared the edge amid a throat-choking cloud of dirt and dust, he looked back down indecisively. "Maybe we can get them out too," he began. "We could—"

"Xander, there's no *time.*" Anya pulled on his arm. "If you have any chance at all of convincing Willow not to do this, we need to go *now.* If not, don't bother to save Buffy and Dawn—or, for that matter, *me.* We'll all be dead in another half hour, anyway!"

He opened his mouth to argue, then closed it with a snap. "Go to Giles," he told her. "If I can't convince her, maybe between the two of you, you can try to find a way to at least . . . I don't know, make it not so bad."

"But—"

"Why are you arguing when you said we don't have time?"

"Oh, all *right,*" she grumbled. "Giles *is* by himself. Oz took off hours ago, and Spike disappeared—we don't have a clue where he went. But you and I—"

"Shhhhh!" He grabbed her and kissed her before she could finish. "Just go!"

With a last, unhappy glance at him, Anya winked out of sight and Xander turned and ran as fast as he could toward Kingman's Bluff.

Chapter Twenty-One

Buffy watched Xander and Anya disappear from sight, then she and Dawn were left to stare upward at a circle of sky—showing the faintest traces of the coming dawn—that had never looked so far away.

"Gee," Dawn said. "It sure would've been great if Xander had tied that rope to a tree or something and dropped it back down here, or maybe if Anya had stayed to get *us* out too."

Buffy shrugged and pulled her gaze away from that tantalizing but too far away escape route. "Like I told him, if he doesn't stop Willow, it's not going to matter anyway. And Giles is alone—at least you and I have each other."

"A nice thought," Dawn said smartly, then pointed at something behind Buffy. "And we have *them,* too."

Buffy turned, expecting the worse. What she saw

pretty much fell into that category—the lumps and bumps along the underground tomb's floor were twisting and turning, pulling themselves up and into walking warriors of the dead. It wasn't exactly heartening when she saw that several of the things were even armed with swords—wasn't that always the way, here in Sunnydale?

"I guess this is Willow's going-away gift," Dawn said as she backed away. Buffy only grimaced as the first of the creatures, a weird cross between a skeleton and some kind of earthen monster, lumbered toward them. Another burst from the wall right behind it, and Dawn couldn't suppress a scream; the thing was made of everything organic: dirt, rocks, roots, tar, and the remains of long-buried bodies. More frightening were the bony protrusions, like blades, sticking out from the ends of their arms, clicking together menacingly, like mutated lobster claws.

"Well," Buffy said with false brightness. "Better now than never!" She rushed the first two of the creatures, levering herself up and into a flying kick at the last instant. They stumbled backward, and she used their sod-bodies as steps to launch herself into a backward flip; when she landed, Buffy saw her chance to snatch at a spare sword embedded in the ground. She pulled it free and brought it up just in time to stop what would have been a decapitating blow, then began to fight in earnest, thrusting back and forth, slashing at anything that moved within her range. The first one tried to attack again and she deftly did the slice-and-dice; it went down in pieces as she turned her hip over into a powerful roundhouse kick that shattered the thigh bones of both the second creature's legs.

"Buffy!"

So much for having time to appreciate her handiwork. She whirled at the sound of Dawn's panicked scream and saw a third earth monster almost on her sister, its blade extended and headed straight for Dawn's face. Buffy kept spinning; her next kick had all her body weight behind it and caught the dead thing smack in the side of the head with enough force to knock it completely off its feet. It went down with its head flopping and its neck broken, and it didn't get back up.

But off to the side, a fourth monster was pulling itself free of the wall, growling and screaming as though it was going through a painful birthing process.

Dawn gasped. "What are you fighting here, the ground?"

Buffy glared at the thing a few feet away and positioned herself solidly in front of her sister. "Looks that way," she said.

"Uh-oh, there's another one!" Dawn jabbed a finger to her other side.

Buffy's lips tightened over her teeth. "I can't take them all," she told her sister. "They just keep coming." She wiped her mouth with the back of her hand, then turned to look at Dawn. "Dawn . . ." Her sister's eyes widened when Buffy offered her the sword she'd picked up earlier. "Will you help me?"

Dawn stared at the weapon in her hand for a moment—a very *short* moment—then raised her gaze to meet Buffy's. "I got your back," she said simply.

Buffy smiled faintly and nodded, then reached down to grab the sword that had fallen from the creature whose neck she'd broken. With her expression twisted in concentration, she turned back to face the thing lumbering toward her; out of the corner of her eye, Buffy saw Dawn inhale, then grip the handle of her sword decisively and head toward the newest monster being born.

If it hadn't been for the fact that her world had been shattered the night before, Willow might have thought the upcoming morning was shaping up to be a beautiful thing.

But no—as she'd stood there, making her final decision to do this last, irreversible act, all she could think about were two photographs back in the loft. One she had packed away in a box, but it was a telling thing that she'd never actually thrown it out, wasn't it? It was a photo of her and Buffy and Xander, the core of the Scooby Gang, dating back years ago, before Tara, before Dawn and all the in-betweens. The other, of course, was of her and Tara in happier times, taken before she'd fallen under Rack's magick drug spell and wasted way too much of what little time she hadn't realized that she and Tara had left. But all those things were gone now—Buffy and Xander would never forgive her for the things she'd done: murder, sacrifice, *evil*. And Tara was out of reach forever—even her spirit, so beautiful and clean and good, had moved on to a place that Willow, because of the darkness within her, could no longer believe she would actually see.

So that was it—everything was kaput. There was nothing left in the world that was good, she had no true friends, she had no light, no *love.* Without Tara, there was simply *nothing,* and if there was no way for Tara to return to her, then where was the reason that the world should go on? So *other* people could be happy and she couldn't? Not even that—she could *feel* all the pain surrounding her now, all the misery that the population of the earth just kept adding to, never stopping, never even *slowing.* It was kind of ironic, really; if Yama thought she had sacrificed everything to get Tara back, wait until he saw what she was going to sacrifice because she *couldn't.*

Willow faced the horizon at Kingman's Bluff and raised her hands, feeling like she was bearing the weight of the world on them. Yes, her power had drained in her fight with Yama, but she was already recharged and ready for this utterly different act.

The ground in front of her swelled, then buckled. Cracks razored across the ground as the earth below churned and rumbled and finally gave up what had been hidden for so many decades. The first thing to push from the soil was the dilapidated spire of a rotted-out steeple; it came out at an impossibly crooked angle, shaking and spilling dirt from every crevice of the hideous gargoyles mounted at each of its jutting ledges.

Watching it rise, Willow reached within herself and found power, more power, always, sent it toward the steeple and *pulled.* Streaks of mystical energy zigzagged from her body and surrounded the bluff and the old building, and she could feel her eyes and hair deepening from black to blacker with the effort of lifting a full-size structure from the bowels of the soil that had swallowed it for so many years.

And finally, there it was.

Against the lovely looking small-town backdrop of Sunnydale, the temple was as tilted as the Tower of Pisa. But it would still serve its purpose, oh yes. The building itself rose at least thirty feet in the air, really nothing but a huge shrine to the image at its base. At the bottom of the temple, Proserpexa's scarred and cracked likeness was akin to something out of a nightmare— she was a Medusa-like she-demon with snakes for hair and forked tongues protruding from two snarling mouths rimmed with multiple rows of razor-sharp teeth . . . the same mouths that seemed to be leering with anticipation at what was coming.

Willow took a deep, mind-clearing breath, pulling in the clean air of the countryside just outside Sunnydale. When her words spilled forth, they sounded deep and guttural, as though someone, or *something* else were using her body to speak.

"*Deinde barathrum excido umbra, excieo Soror Tenebrae! Excieo!* From the pit of forgotten shadows, awake, Sister of the Dark! Awaken!"

The earth beneath her feet rumbled again, this time all around her. The steeple pitched slightly to the left but it held, and the effigy's eyes suddenly blazed with scarlet light and burned into Willow's black gaze.

"*Proserpexa,*" she continued, "*effreno purgo*

deflagratio deinde umbra, cremo aboleo perpessio anima, adgero dulcesco mortifer. Proserpexa, let the cleansing fires from the depths burn away the suffering souls, and bring sweet death. . . ."

The serene, pink light of dawn that had been seeping into the day was suddenly washed over with black-and-purple electricity. It traveled through the air in jagged arcs, bouncing from Willow's fingertips to the waiting, hungry effigy, then it ran back to Willow and surrounded her, swirling around and around and consuming her, until it all came out—

Her eyes.

The power poured out of her in a single, concentrated beam, and it went right back into the effigy, funneling itself into only one purpose: to bring Proserpexa's power back to existence and destroy the world. The statue soaked it up like it was a sponge rather than stone, its gray surface gradually warming to red and heading for the same crimson hue as its eyes. Each second that passed increased its heat and made it look darker and more sinister.

Willow felt like she was spinning and floating and falling all at the same time, yet she was still solidly bound to the earth, still maintained her balance and, above all, her purpose. She threw her head back and went with the feeling, letting it take control of her as she narrowed her blackened eyes to slits but never let Proserpexa's image out of her sight.

The ground beneath her rumbled and twisted itself into an earthquake. The earth at the base of the effigy suddenly turned black in a circle around it; a moment

later the edges of that circle blazed red, like paper sur-
rendering itself to the beauty of fire. The circle began
to spread outward and swallow more ground, at first
creeping, then spreading more and more quickly. It
was almost a third down the mound of earth on which
the temple sat when—

Xander stepped between Willow's power beam
and the image of Proserpexa.

She and Dawn were looking at yet another duo of earth
monsters dragging themselves into existence when
Buffy nearly lost her footing as another of a series of
earthquakes rumbled through the ground. A cloud of
dirt, dust, and rocks tumbled from the darker area of
the ceiling, lumping into soft piles that no doubt would
soon form themselves into animated adversaries.

While that was true enough, it was the *cause* of the
earthquakes that worried Buffy more. "Willow," she
muttered to herself, then ran her sword up the arm of
one of the creatures as it tried to lunge at her.

Buffy spun to protect herself from the rear and saw
Dawn go into a defensive crouch against her own foe,
swiping at it and cutting away mostly useless bits and
pieces of dirt and wood. She paid for her timidness
when the dirt-beast swung forward and sliced deeply
into her upper arm. To Buffy's dismay, her sister
screamed and reflexively dropped her sword.

"Dawn—I'm coming!"

Buffy arced her sword over her head and lopped
off the arm of the creature nearest to her, then had to
fall back as another one joined forces with the one she

was fighting. Her heart was hammering as she saw Dawn's monster reach for her, those nasty bone-things at the ends of its arms clicking in anticipation.

Not acceptable.

With renewed determination, Buffy ducked under the blade coming toward her at head level, then spun, bringing her sword around backward, up, then down again in a sort of open-ended figure eight. Both the creatures attacking her looked at her with strangely surprised expressions, then doubled over and collapsed. She whirled to run to Dawn—

—and saw her sister drop into an excellent dive-and-roll past the beast trying to grab at her. Dawn snatched up her dropped sword, and as the monster turned toward her, she thrust it into the thing's midsection, twisting the blade to get the fullest damage effect. As Buffy stared, stunned, Dawn yanked the sword free, then swung it again, neatly decapitating her assailant. The now-headless monster wobbled there for a moment, then fell at her feet with a meaty thud.

Panting, Dawn frowned at it, then lifted her gaze to meet that of her speechless sister. "What?" she finally demanded. "You think I never watched you?"

"Well," Buffy began, "I—"

Whatever else Buffy was going to say was forgotten as another two of the earthen creatures pulled themselves free of the tomb's dirt walls and headed straight for them, forcing her and Dawn to back up until they were spine to spine, with their swords poised as they made ready to fight for their lives. . . .

• • •

"There," Giles whispered.

Anya looked over from where she'd been standing at the Magic Box's front window and staring out at the street. It was here that she'd decided to come to face the end of the world, knowing that Giles would also be here, always searching for another way to save humanity even when he already knew it was fruitless. "What?"

From across the room where he was sitting at the table amid a jumble of ancient books, Giles looked up and smiled faintly. Anya got the distinct feeling he was seeing something that wasn't at all in the room. "It's not over," he said softly.

The building suddenly trembled, and plaster dust sifted down on them. Anya looked up at the ceiling, then at the floor as another of the small earthquakes that had been going on for the last quarter hour rumbled underneath, etching a jagged crack in front of her feet to mark its passing. Anya's gaze was dark when she looked back at him. "I don't know if I believe that," she finally said. "But I suppose we'll figure it out in another fifteen minutes."

Chapter Twenty-Two

"**H**ey, black-eyed girl," Xander said in his best everyday hanging-out conversation voice. Behind him, the nearly redhot image of the she-demon began to fade almost immediately, its lava-colored surface rapidly cooling as the contact with Willow and her power source was broken and the energy dissipated. "Whatcha doing?"

Willow blinked. With her concentration destroyed, her eyes returned to their normal color again, and she stared at Xander incredulously. "Get *out* of here!"

Xander shoved his hands in his pockets and gave an almost shy shrug, then jabbed his thumb at himself. "You're not the only one with powers, you know. You may be a hopped-up überwitch, but this carpenter can drywall you into the next century."

"I'm not joking, Xander. Get out of my way. *Now*."

She jerked one hand at him, and Xander was abruptly thrown backward. He slammed against the base of the statue with bone-cracking force, gasping as he tried to breathe around the pain and rolling on the scorched earth. With sudden, fierce focus, Willow's eyes went black again and her brow furrowed, but not before a look of remorse skittered across her face. Once again, she drew the energy from herself and sent it into Proserpexa, feeding it everything she could.

The ground rocked again, but Xander dragged himself forward, holding on to his ribs and sucking air through his clenched teeth. Before another earthquake could gather momentum, he forced himself to his feet, staggered forward a couple of steps—

—and again blocked the flow of power from Willow to the statue.

Willow's hands dropped to her sides, and she scowled at him. "You can't stop this."

"Yeah," Xander said. His words were strained. "I get that. It's just . . . where else am I going to go? You've been my best friend my whole life. World's gonna end, so where else would I want to be when it does?"

It was so unbelievable, Willow rolled her eyes and almost laughed. "Is this your great master plan? You're going to stop me by telling me you love me?!"

He gave her one of his crooked grins. "Well, I was going to walk you off a cliff and hand you an anvil, but it seemed kind of cartoony."

Her urge to laugh whispered away. "Still making jokes," she said softly.

But Xander shook his head. "I'm not joking. I know you're in pain. I can't imagine the pain you're going through. I also know you're about to do something apocalyptically evil and stupid, but hey, I still want to hang. You're Willow."

Willow's eyes blazed. "Don't call me th—"

"The first day of kindergarten," Xander continued, "you cried because you broke the yellow crayon and you were too afraid to tell anyone. You've come pretty far, ending the world and all that. Not a terrific notion, I'll grant you—but yeah. I love you. I loved crayon-breaking Willow and I love scary, veiny Willow. So if I'm going out, it's here, with you. You want to kill the world? Then start with me. I've been through a lot because of you, *for* you, and I've earned that number-one slot."

She curled her fingers into fists, felt the too-sharp ends of her fingernails digging furrows into her palms. "You think I won't?" she demanded.

Xander only looked at her. "It doesn't matter," he said simply. "I'll still love you."

"Shut *UP*!" she screamed. One hand lashed out and made a clawing motion in the air between them. Xander winced as three large cuts opened in the flesh of one cheek. He reached up and touched the blood trickling from the wounds, then studied the red liquid on his fingers. He shook his head, dismissing it, and his eyes found hers again. "I love you," he repeated.

Willow snarled and slashed at the air again; this time his shirt split open across one shoulder as larger, deeper wounds bit into flesh and muscle. Now the pain was almost enough to double him over, but he wouldn't go, he wouldn't fall. Not until he told her again. "I love—"

Willow squeezed her eyes shut and blasted him with an energy bolt, nearly wailing with regret. This time he did go down, crying out as his back hit the ground and the ends of the ribs broken by Willow's first attack pushed at one another. One shoulder of his shirt was soaked with blood, but it didn't matter—he still staggered back to his feet and headed toward her. "I . . . *love* you."

"Shut up!" Willow cried.

She blasted him again, and while he grunted in pain, this time there wasn't quite enough behind the blow to knock him down. "I love you, Willow," he said. There wasn't much volume to his voice, but there didn't have to be: She heard the words loud and clear.

"Stop," she whimpered. She gestured at him, but this time her wave of energy barely registered at all. Now he was there and reaching for her, and she tried to hit him with her fists, shaking her head violently—

No no no no no—

—but he didn't care. She could hit him from now until the end of the world, until *she* ended the world, and it wouldn't change how he felt about her. He didn't care how much pain he was in, or how much pain he had endured in the past; he didn't even care if she had been the cause of it. All he cared about was Willow.

And Willow could *feel* that, she could. Her knees buckled, and Xander knelt down with her, holding her and rocking her as she covered her hands with her eyes and wailed in agony, cried for everything she'd lost and everything she'd caused, and for all the things she couldn't change or fix or undo. The more she cried, the more she changed—her black hair slipped back to red, the darkness leaked out of her eyes, the black, spidery veins beneath her skin twisted away into nothingness.

Until, finally, the old Willow that Xander had loved and been terrified he'd lost forever, was back.

"I love you," he said again. And while she cried, he held her tightly as the final glow in the effigy of Proserpexa burned away to stone-cold gray.

Buffy and Dawn felt each other tense as at least four more of the dirt creatures surrounded them. Bony hand-claws clattering, the creatures bared teeth laced with soil and reached for them—

Then froze.

They leered at the two women, then suddenly all four of them howled in pain and brought their over-developed hands up to clutch at their own heads. Their screeches went on and on as Buffy and Dawn gaped at them, then abruptly every last one of the monsters collapsed into mounds of harmless dirt and rocks.

"What happened?" Dawn asked in bewilderment.

She didn't answer right away, but Buffy had an idea about that. A very *good* idea.

"Satisfied yet?"

Anya hugged herself, then glanced around at the Magic Box suspiciously, as if she expected the floor and the building to start shaking again at any moment.

"I . . ." She pressed her lips together. Finally, she demanded, "Why aren't you dead? Why aren't *I* dead?"

Giles's expression was pleased. "Because the threat's gone—Willow's been stopped."

Anya's eyes widened, and she stopped striding back and forth long enough to gape at him. "You mean she's—"

But Giles only smiled. "She's alive. The magick she took from me, it did what I hoped it would."

Her mouth dropped open as realization sank in. "Wait—you *dosed* her! You *knew* she was going to take your powers all along!"

"W-well . . ." He hesitated, then decided to continue. "I knew there was a *possibility* that would happen. The gift I was given by the coven was the true essence of Magick, which comes, in all its purity, from the earth itself. Willow's magick came from a place of rage and power—"

"Oh, there was rage, all right," Anya cut in. She gave him a knowing look. "And vengeance. Don't forget vengeance."

Giles's hand went involuntarily to his stomach. "How could I?" He shook his head, as though trying to dislodge the bad memories of being the Gnarl's dinner item and leave them behind. "In any case, the magick she took from me tapped into the spark of humanity she had left. It took a while—it took *Xander* and his determination to get through to her, but it finally allowed her to once more feel something besides vengeance."

Anya frowned. "Xander?"

Giles nodded. "Yes, Xander. He was the one who

got to her in time." He let that sink in, then added, "He saved us all, you know."

Anya thought about that. Wow—Xander had . . . well, he'd been the hero of the day and had succeeded in saving the world. How cool was that?

Pretty darned good for a carpenter.

"I . . . I think it's over, Buffy. The world's still here."

Still in a battle crouch, Buffy eyed the cavern suspiciously. A beam of sunlight was just spilling over the edge of the overhead hole; a heavy layer of dust motes floated within the steam of light, but nothing else moved. Finally she let the sword slip out of her hand, then sank to her knees. She was *exhausted,* completely drained by the fight. Not just tonight's, but the ones over the previous weeks, where sometimes she'd won—against vampires—and, as with Willow and that awful cat-demon, often she'd lost. But at the end of it all, at least the world hadn't come to an end. She didn't want to—she didn't at all want Dawn to see this—but she just couldn't stop herself from putting her face in her hands and weeping.

Her sister stared at her for a moment, then frowned and lifted her chin. "Hey, sorry to disappoint," she began, then stopped. "Wait . . . is that . . . happy crying?"

Through her tears, Buffy felt herself smile. "Yeah, dummy—you think I *wanted* the world to end?"

"I didn't know," Dawn said uncertainly. "Didn't you?"

Buffy stared at her. "Dawn, I'm so sorry," she said softly. She pushed herself to her feet, then pulled

Dawn into a hug. The tears started again, and this time she hid her face against Dawn's shoulder.

"It's okay, Buffy." Dawn held on to her, feeling her own eyes start to sting. "It's okay—"

"No, it hasn't been. It hasn't been okay." Buffy pulled back, then touched Dawn's cheek. "But it's going to be. I see that now." She stepped away and wiped her cheeks with the back of one hand, then went over to one of at least half a dozen coffins that had fallen out of the dirt walls during the course of their battle with the earth monsters. Getting a solid grip on one end, she began to drag the wooden box toward the center of the cavern to a place directly beneath the hole overhead.

"See what?" Dawn asked, confused.

Buffy smiled. "You," she said, as she kept working. "Things have sucked lately, but it's all going to change, and I want to *be* there when it does. I want to see my friends happy again." She glanced sideways at Dawn, and her voice got thick. "And I want to see you grow up, the woman you're going to become . . . because she's going to be *beautiful*."

Dawn stared at her, but she couldn't think of anything to say. A tear escaped from the corner of one eye and made its way slowly down the curve of her cheek.

"And she's going to be powerful," Buffy continued. "I had it so *wrong*. I don't want to protect you from the world. I want to *show* it to you!" She stopped pulling on the dilapidated coffins long enough to cup Dawn's face in her grubby hands. "Oh, Dawn—there's so much I want to show you."

Dawn blinked and felt more tears spill from her

eyes, but she couldn't suppress a grin. "Don't you think we ought to get out of this hole first?"

The sun had just crested the horizon when Buffy finally managed to get a solid hold on a tree root just over the edge of the hole. It had taken an impressive pile of rotting coffins, dirt, rocks, bones, and whatever other kind of debris they could find to make a tottering tower high enough for her to climb to get up there. Once there, she had an unpleasant ten seconds where it looked like her unstable perch was going to drop her right on her butt and make them start over; at the last second, Buffy's scrabbling fingers found purchase and she was able to steady herself.

She hauled herself up and out of the hole, glanced around, then turned and held out her hand to Dawn. A few moments later she had a solid hold on her sister and pulled her free of the underground tomb. The two of them squinted at the bright sun, then clambered to their feet and brushed the dirt and twigs from their clothes. When her eyes had adjusted, Buffy suddenly realized what she was seeing just past Dawn's slender figure.

Dawn stepped up beside her and Buffy threw her arm over her sister's shoulder. They were on a hill, just one of many. Before them, under a lovely blue sky on an uncharacteristically springlike day, was a rolling vista of green grass and trees, and not far in the distance and looking more welcoming than it had in years, was their own little town of Sunnydale.

Smiling at each other, they took their first steps toward home.

Epilogue

The truck bounced and swayed and clacked, despite the fact that they were driving on a fairly smooth highway. Jonathan and Andrew gritted their teeth and tried not to think about the seedy-looking driver who'd picked them up about seventy miles back. God only knew when he'd bathed last or washed his clothes, and he was chewing away on a wad of tobacco. Every few minutes he'd spit a black gob of juice into an empty soda can he'd precariously balanced on the dashboard. That was bad enough, but both guys found the wet, black streaks dripping down his chin and onto his gritty, stained flannel shirt utterly horrifying.

Unfortunately, this guy was only the latest in a series of truckers who'd been generous enough to offer rides to the two tired and terrified hitchhikers headed into Mexico, but each driver seemed to look worse,